Blackworth

by Patrick Ament

ISBN-13: 9781234567890
ISBN-10: 1477123456

Cover design by: Schmelling Design
Library of Congress Control Number: 2018675309
Printed in the United States of America

Table of Contents

Chapter 1: Lord Blackworth, pt. I................................4
Chapter 2: Gwenli, pt. I......................................8
Chapter 3: Aelos 13
Chapter 4: Lord Blackworth, pt. II............................22
Chapter 5: Darkness...26
Chapter 6: Isra and Anroth.....................................35
Chapter 7: Grandpa and Grandma............................42
Chapter 8: Declaration 47
Chapter 9: Gwenli, pt. II.......................................52
Chapter 10: Lief..58
Chapter 11: Magerson Who Broke His Trace........64
Chapter 12: Enthcas...69
Chapter 13: Pentelaud..75
Chapter 14: Aunt Estaia's House 80
Chapter 15: Light 89
Chapter 16: Ceremony..96
Chapter 17: Darkness, pt. II 101
Chapter 18: Persevere...108
Chapter 19: Lord Blackworth, pt. III.....................113
APPENDIX: LIST OF CELESTIM.....................115

Chapter 1
Lord Blackworth, pt. I

"Lord Blackworth, we must push forward! The city is nearly ours!"

He spun, the clamor of battle ringing in his ears. The voice belonged to his most trusted advisor, Alistair, whose long white hair, the mark of a lifetime bachelor, was stained red with blood.

Blackworth nodded and thrust his longsword high into the air. "Forward, men!" With a cry, he charged towards the city gates.

The city of Enthcas's glittering walls and towers shone in the morning sky. Blackworth's home, occupied by enemy soldiers. The great citadel had been overtaken by the evil warlord General Gripper. But now, Blackworth and his band of loyal soldiers, the Great Hundred, had come to take back their home.

And victory was in sight.

Enemy soldiers saw his charge. They stepped into his path, but Blackworth was like wind. Here and then gone. The point of his sword danced like lightning, piercing flesh with every stroke.

Alistair's voice came again from behind. "My lord, the general! He's here!"

Blackworth looked up and saw, indeed, the great enemy general was standing in front of the city gates. Gripper wore black plate armor and carried a heavy iron mace.

Gripper's men gave a great shout at the sight of their leader. The fighting had ceased, and the enemy forces stood on the balls of their feet as he began to stride towards the battlefield.

Blackworth pushed forward through the men and called out, "General, you have fought well today! Or rather, your army has fought well. I was disappointed not to have seen you leading the charge with your men!"

The remaining members of Blackworth's Great Hundred laughed. Gripper's men growled, bristling at the insult to their leader. Gripper himself continued to stride forward and smiled easily. "The fight is not over yet, boy." He spat the last with contempt, his thick accent slurring the words together.

"Boy?" Blackworth frowned in mock confusion. "I'm flattered, Gripper, but I'm almost as old as you— though not nearly half as wide." Behind him, the Great Hundred laughed again.

Gripper ignored him. "I challenge you," the large man called, "to death-ending combat. Whoever wins takes the city."

Blackworth felt a hand on his shoulder. "My lord, I—"

"Alistair, please," he shrugged. The white-haired man had been Blackworth's closest advisor since he was a boy, but he still didn't approve of Blackworth's 'fight first, talk second' approach to leadership.

Lord Blackworth turned back to Gripper and raised his blade in response. "Accepted, General. Let's begin!"

Gripper waved Blackworth on and brought his mace up in a two-handed, defensive stance.

I'm smaller and faster than him, he thought. *I can use that.* Blackworth charged forward, closing the distance in seconds. In a flash, the young lord swung, Gripper barely deflecting it with one of his great iron bracers.

Behind him, Blackworth's men cheered him on. Gripper scowled and shifted his weight, swinging his mace in a vicious counterattack.

Blackworth leapt aside, but his heel caught on a stray stone and he stumbled backwards. The black-iron mace scraped along his shoulder and knocked him to the ground.

Behind him, the men of his battalion cried out in shock. He managed to scramble to his feet quickly, but his ears rang and his shoulder burned with pain.

Now it was Gripper's turn to taunt. "Come, boy. Let's fight some more. I'm rather liking this!"

Blackworth rolled his arm experimentally and forced a smirk. "Likewise!" He darted forward and swung his sword up towards Gripper's helmet.

Again, the armored man batted the attack away and countered, but this time Blackworth was prepared. When the mace came from the left, Blackworth dropped his longsword, leapt up into the air and launched himself high onto Gripper's shoulders.

The general cried out in shock, nearly losing his balance. "What are you—"

In one motion, Blackworth drew his belt-knife and slit the general's throat from above. Gripper's cries turned to desperate, suffocated gurgles as the young lord kicked off of him to land in a crouch, catching his longsword just above the dirt.

The field went silent as the great general toppled forward into the dirt.

Blackworth wiped his face and brandished his blade. "This city is ours!" he cried to the enemy soldiers. "Leave now, or face execution!"

Gripper's men blinked.

"Your general is defeated! Return to your homeland!"

Clouds of dust rose as they ran from his home.

"My lord, we are successfully returned, but we must still account for—"

"I don't want to think about it now, Alistair," Blackworth interrupted. "Let me celebrate! I'm home again, and so are you. Why can't you just relax?" Together, they walked down the halls of the royal keep, where Blackworth had grown up and now ruled from.

Alistair smirked. "Trust me, my lord, we don't want that. If I relax, who would be here to remind you about—"

"No, no, none of it," Blackworth cut him off. "Tonight is a night for celebration!"

"You would not be a good ruler if you did not at least give it *some* thought."

"Then I suppose I am not a good ruler," he laughed. "Come. There's no need—"

Alistair stopped walking. "Do not be a coward, Ellison."

He flinched. It was rare that anyone addressed him by that name anymore. Blackworth paused. "I'm not a coward. I just...don't want to think of it."

"It's your Trace. It determines how you live the rest of your life!" Alistair exclaimed.

Alistair's voice was...different. The world was dissolving, Lord Blackworth was slipping away. "So?"

"So what?" Ellison snapped.

"So what? So what are you going to pick?"

What are you going to pick?

The question had taken hold, and it was pulling him back to reality. The escape was only temporary—the pleasures of a boyish daydream. Lord Blackworth was dissipating, and Ellison, the fourteen-year-old boy, was left in his place.

Chapter 2
Gwenli, pt. I

"—going to pick? Ell? Ellison? Hello?"

The daydream was already dissolved, replaced by reality. Lord Blackworth and Alistair were left behind, just a figment of the young boy's imagination, as was General Gripper and his bloodthirsty army. No longer were there grand battles to fight or victory feasts to attend—just the dullness of step, step, step, step.

It was hard not to get lost in imaginary things when you travelled in a caravan like Ellison's. The days in the cities were plenty of work, but for every day with a nice warm bed and cobblestone streets, there were ten in between where the only thing for a young boy like Ellison to do was walk and think.

There were about ten families in their caravan, perhaps forty people, all led by Ell's father. Papa was a good leader, Ellison thought, and he always rode the family wagon at the front of the caravan—*so I'm the first to encounter any trouble,* he'd explained.

"Hello? Ellison Blackworth, where are you? Snap out of it!"

The voice belonged to Ell's best friend, Gwenli. Her family had been with the caravan as long as his, and they'd been close since birth.

"What, Gwen?" asked Ell, releasing the last vestiges of his imaginary life. He'd return to Lord Blackworth and Alistair later.

She raised her eyebrows. "Well? I asked you what you're going to pick."

"For what?" he frowned, feigning confusion in the hope that maybe she'd give up.

"Oh, my breathing days! For your Trace," she insisted. "You *have* been thinking about it, right? It's sort of a big choice to make."

Ellison stared down at the road. "I'm still thinking. What about you?"

Gwen's eyes lit up and she took a deep breath like she was preparing to dive underwater. "Well, I was thinking Curiosity. It's really the best choice for me, because, well, you know how curious I always am about, really, everything," she giggled, "and you know how my mum always says, 'my Gwen, she'll listen to every conversation you have with her, and every one you don't have with her too,' well," she paused to take another deep breath, "I think that she means that in a bad way, but really I take it as a compliment, because..."

Gwen was a talker. Ell's mother said Gwen talked because she just assumed you were paying attention. *She's a bright girl, Gwenli is. Sometimes I wonder if she's too bright for the rest of us.*

Ellison didn't mind. For all her words, Gwenli was as good a listener as anyone he knew. If you had a story to tell, she was in the front row, mouth shut until you told her you were finished. Gwen remembered the tiniest, most minute details you could mention. She was the only person he knew who could listen passionately.

"...but really, I don't think it's much to worry about. Unless something seriously changes, I think I'll be very curious forever, so you know it's surely the best idea. Do you think so too?"

He shrugged. "I don't know. There are so many choices, I don't...I don't want to make the wrong one."

Ellison's fifteenth birthday was fast approaching, and with it, his Trace Declaration. When the day came, he would stand before his community—the caravan—and declare the Celestial path that he would strive to follow for the rest of his days. There were twenty-three Celestim, twenty-three Traces to choose from. Declaring your Trace was a social rite of passage, but it was also a religious requirement for all Aesekri believers. You could not call yourself a good Aesekri if you did not pick a Trace at fifteen.

"That's understandable. I heard that back when Grandpa Emory was our age, he was so worried about choosing his Trace that he threw up all over the grass right before his Declaration. But—"

"Dedication, perhaps?" he wondered aloud. "I like the idea of being dedicated to something all my life, but what if I get bored? Maybe Vigilance would be good, but that just sounds so...exhausting. Honesty, perhaps."

"Doesn't your papa Trace Honesty?" Gwen asked. "You should ask him for help. At least he'll give you his truthful opinion," she laughed.

Ellison sighed. Gwenli made that particular joke at least once a day. "I've already tried, but he just says I need to be true to myself and choose whatever feels right."

"Then do that," Gwen said as if it cleared everything up. "Look, Ell. The tradition of Traces is as old as Firion himself. Well, maybe not that old. Though I suppose..."

Firion was the God Above All, creator of Reqius and the rest of the Cogniverse. "I get what you mean, Gwen."

"That's not my point, though. My point is, everyone picks a Trace. Thousands of people, maybe a million. Maybe even more than that!"

"Not people who aren't Aesekri," Ell mumbled.

"Don't be difficult, Ellison Blackworth," Gwen shot back, folding her arms. "Every person who's called themselves an Aesekri, since the beginning of the ages, has declared a Trace on their fifteenth birthday."

"What's your point?"

"Well, don't you think you'll be able to do the same? Everyone else has done it. Going by the odds, you'll be fine, right?"

Ellison frowned. "I doubt *everyone's* done it."

She paused. "No, you're probably right. Sorry, that didn't help as much as I thought it would."

"It's fine, Gwen. Thanks. I'm just going to see if Mum and Papa have any advice," Ellison said. "We have a prayer or so until the Declaration, don't we?"

"Two prayers, one week, and three days," Gwen nodded.

The largest moon over Reqius took thirty-odd days to go from full to full again. The morning after every full moon was a morning for prayer—a time for Aesekri believers to pray to the patron Celestim of their Trace. Prayers came about every thirty days. Fifteen prayers in a year, five weeks in a prayer, five days in a week. It was the same calendar system used across most of Reqius.

"...and I was talking to my father about it today, and he said that mine and your Declarations are going to be held on the same night, since our birthdays are so close to each other."

"That might be nice," he said. "That way, not all of the focus will be on just me. I can split it with you." Ellison and Gwenli were born two days apart from each other. Gwenli was the oldest of three girls, while Ell was his parents' only child.

11

"I'm excited. There's always a big celebration after Declarations, and my father said this one would be even bigger since it's for the two of us together."

"I'm excited for it," Ellison lied. "Do you know how far we are from the city?" The caravan would be arriving in the city of Aelos by the end of the day.

"Less than an hour," Gwen said. "If you run up over that hill you can see it. Wanna go?"

Before Ellison could reply, he heard Papa's voice shout down the caravan from the leading wagon. "City in sight!" The men in the other families echoed the call backwards, passing the message along down the line.

Gwenli beamed. "Already! Come on, let's get to the front. Maybe we can ride in your papa's wagon!"

Chapter 3
Aelos

They made their way up to Papa's wagon and asked if they could ride with him into Aelos. He shifted to the left, making space for Gwenli and Ell to sit. "Look," Gwenli pointed as they climbed up. "You can see some of the buildings already!"

"Do you see that big one at the center?" said Papa, adjusting his hold on the reins. "That's Castle Firalos."

"Really?" Gwenli gasped. "Where the Monarchs live?"

Papa nodded. "Indeed. It was built on a hill at the center of the city, so that all of Aelos would slope up towards it. People say that Aelos literally looks to its leaders."

"Can we go there?" asked Gwenli.

"No," said Papa. "Ordinary people can't go there. Only important ones, like the Monarchs."

She sighed. "I want to see it."

"Who knows?" Papa laughed. "Maybe you will one day." Up ahead lay the city gates, and Aelos behind them. "Alright," he said, snapping the reins. "Lesson time! Today's lesson…oh, let's see. Any questions,

either of you? Yes, Gwen, you always have questions—
Ell, what about you?"

The adults of the caravan were very serious about
making sure their children received an adequate, well-
rounded education. *A good trader knows a little bit of
everything,* Mum always said. It was quite normal for any
one of the adults to spring an impromptu educatory
session on Ellison or Gwen or one of the other children
at any time.

Ellison shrugged. "I don't think so."

"I've got one," Gwen chirped.

Papa chuckled. "Alright then, let's hear it."

"I was thinking about something this morning. I
know the story of the five Celestim who turned evil,
who hurt Firion. They were cast out of Celestia, right?"

Papa nodded. "The Celestim were created to help
rule the Cogniverse—twenty-eight, all serving under
Firion. Each one embodied a certain trait or emotion.
Love, Lust, Perseverance, Ambition—you've
memorized them all by now. One day long ago, five of
them, led by the Celestim of Submission, tried to kill
Firion and take his place as above all things. They got
close, but in the end, they only crippled him. In return,
Firion cast them down to worlds they once governed.
They are called the Nirrin, and now they wander the
Cogniverse doing evil."

"Right, right," said Gwen. "People used to Trace
them, didn't they? Before they were evil, I mean."

"Submission, Terror, Rage, Lust, and Ambition,"
Papa recounted. "Yes, when they were Celestim, people
Traced them."

Gwen frowned. "Can they still?"

Papa's face darkened immediately. "Why do you ask
that?"

"I'm just curious," she shrugged.

"Yes, my girl. They can."

"Do you know anyone who's ever tried to do that?" she asked.

"No," Papa answered, his voice low. "Gwen, this is a dark subject. I don't think you should bring it up to anyone else, alright?"

Gwenli frowned. "Er—okay." There was only a momentary silence before she spoke again. "Why not?"

Papa sighed. "Let me explain something to both of you. I'm sure you've heard it before, but it bears repeating, especially as your Declarations are fast approaching."

Ellison watched his father's face, but the man was almost unreadable. For someone who Traced Honesty, he did an excellent job of masking his emotions.

"After Firion's Crippling, the remaining Celestim began to govern the Cogniverse. Each of them embodies a specific emotion or trait. Peace, for example, or Love or Honesty. At age fifteen, all those who recognize the Celestim as the true undergods of the Cogniverse, those who call themselves Aesekri, stand before their community and declare which Celestial path, of the twenty-three, they will Trace. When you choose a Trace, you're choosing which of the twenty-three you want to be tied to for forever." He must've seen the look on Ellison's face at this because he immediately added, "It's okay to be nervous, son. I'd be more concerned if you weren't."

Ell took a deep breath and nodded. "It's okay, Papa. I'm fine."

"Now, a lot of young children understand that the Trace Declaration is an important decision," Papa continued. "Your Trace will influence every decision you make if you follow it well. But there is a greater incentive to keeping your Trace."

"True Victory," Gwen supplied.

"Exactly, my girl. When I was your age, I chose to Trace Honesty. Now, if I Trace Honesty very, very

15

well—if I am the most Honest person to ever hold my Trace, when I die, I become the Celestim of Honesty. My spirit would ascend to Celestia and I would take on the undergod's duties, privileges, and powers. This is what all Aesekri aim to achieve, but only very few ever succeed in."

Gwen frowned. "So you're saying that right now, the Celestim of Honesty used to be a regular person? Like one of us?"

Papa nodded.

"Hmm. I never thought of it like that," she hummed.

"What happens to the rest of us?" Ellison asked. "Those who don't achieve the True Victory?"

"It is said that those who follow their Traces well, but not to the point of True Victory, are reborn as citizens of Celestia and live there forever," Papa explained. "Not so bad. Now, today's lesson is over. There was something else I wanted to talk to the two of you about before we get into the city."

Ellison frowned. His father hadn't answered Gwenli's question about Tracing the Nirrinic paths. "Papa, you didn't tell us—"

"That's enough, Ellison," his father snapped. "I said the lesson is over. Is that understood?"

He flushed. "Yes, Papa."

Gwen shot him a confused glance, but Ell didn't say anything. His father was not usually so harsh—something must've been amiss.

"Tomorrow is sell-day," Papa began.

Gwenli groaned. "I hate sell-day."

Papa laughed, his easygoing demeanor already restored. "Without sell-day, we'd have no way of making profit. We'd be poor as rocks."

"It's so boring," she sighed. "We can't even do anything all day."

Papa smiled. "That's just what I wanted to mention. You're both getting quite old. Drast, you'll be fifteen in two prayers. I talked with your parents, Gwen, and we've agreed that starting tomorrow, we'd like you to begin training as traders yourselves."

The children both glanced at each other, confused. "What do you mean?" Ellison asked.

"You're going to begin learning how to sell," he explained. "How to bargain, set deals, all of it. And then, maybe one day, you two could run your own wagon."

Ellison's eyebrows shot up, and he locked eyes with Gwenli. "Really?"

Papa smiled. "Of course, it's going to be a while before then. Tomorrow, Gwen, you'll start training at your parents' wagon. Ell, you'll be a third trader with Mum and me"

"That's...that's..." Gwen beamed. "I'm going to go tell my pa!" She leapt off the wagon and tore off towards the back of the caravan, where her parents' cart was.

Papa smiled as she ran off. "Are you ready for it, son?"

"I think so," Ell replied.

"I think so too," he smiled. "But I should warn you, they'll try to push you around. They'll think that just because you're young, you're ignorant. Trust me, they did the same to me when I started."

"I won't let them take advantage of me. I'll be brave."

"It takes more than just bravery," Papa said. "It takes perseverance."

Ellison frowned. "What's the difference?"

"Bravery is the ability to do the right thing when you're afraid," he explained. "Perseverance is the ability to do the right thing when it's hard."

He pondered for a few moments, then finally admitted, "I still don't get it."

"Well, sometimes tasks can be overwhelming. Sometimes there are people who don't want to see you succeed. They'll try to discourage you or break you down."

"Hmm." Ellison shifted in his seat. Up ahead, the city gates were rapidly nearing.

They sat in silence for a few moments until suddenly, Papa spoke. "You'll find as you grow up that the hardest opposition comes from your own self-doubt." He paused, then, as if he'd only just realized it, said, "The loudest voice in your ears is often the one between them."

Ellison and his father led the line of wagons smoothly up to the gate. Papa handed Ellison the reins while he went and spoke with the city guards about their caravan.

After a moment, Papa left the guards and hopped back into the wagon, taking the reins back. "It's been too long since I've had a nice bed to sleep on," he said. "Let's go."

They rolled easily through the thick iron gates of Aelos, and then the city was upon them.

A cacophony of sounds assaulted Ellison's ears. The quiet of the road was gone, ripped from him like a rug from under his feet.

He could hear at least two different street performers playing different, clashing melodies, and a dozen beggars calling for coin, their cries harmonizing with the street vendors hawking their wares. The smell of fresh bread and baked sugar apples wafted through the street. The rich dyes and deep colors surrounding him clashed messily with each other. Deep violets, bright oranges, dresses of sackcloth brushing against gossamer. This district of the city didn't seem particularly wealthy to Ellison, but there were a few posh-looking ladies wandering the street in their ornate dresses, their hair braided or down according to age. A few of them glanced over at Ellison and his father as the wagon moved down the street, and he suddenly felt an insuppressible wave of inadequacy regarding his own travel-worn cloak and twice-hemmed pants.

"It's beautiful, isn't it?"

Ellison glanced up and saw that Papa was smiling, his eyes surveying their surroundings with glee. He glanced back at the streets. "I suppose..." There was certainly a kind of allure, a beauty, but not in the traditional sense. Not beautiful like a young bride or a newborn, but beautiful like a massive painting. If you looked too close, you might notice flaws in the brushwork—a crippled beggar child huddled against an alley or a draskim addict twitching violently in the shadows—but as long as you stepped back and saw it from a distance, it was a thing of beauty.

Aelosi streets were wide. In some cities, the caravan's wagons couldn't fit more than one at a time down the causeway. Here, they could've travelled two-by-two and still had room for pedestrians to stroll by.

Less than an hour after they'd entered the city, Papa called for a halt and once more, handed Ell the reigns as he stepped off into a large tavern with a sign painted over the door that read *The Oaken Toast*. When Papa came out the door again, he cupped his hands around his mouth and yelled down the line, "Pack up! Stables four to sixteen, just down the way." Then, he walked beside the wagon, Ellison steering the oxen, and led them down a side street, where a massive stable area had been constructed in conjunction with the tavern they were staying at. The men working there got right to work unharnessing the oxen and guiding them into the pens. After that, Ellison, Papa, and the other men of the caravan worked to push the carts up against the wall.

"That's it, then," said Papa when the last wheels were blocked in place. "Tomorrow is sell-day. We meet in the taproom an hour before dawn. Have a good night, all."

The tavernkeeper provided dinner as arranged and they ate together. After, Ellison and his parents went back to their rooms to settle in.

"Mum? Papa?" he asked, sitting on the edge of their bed. His own bed was a cot on the ground next to them—not fabulous, but better than sleeping on the wagon floor for another night.

"Yes, dear?" his mother replied, looking up from the book she was reading.

"What—I was wondering," he began, "how did—when you picked your Trace, how did you know it was the right one?"

"Well," Papa answered, "For myself, it was relatively simple. I just...looked inside myself and searched for what was true."

There was a moment of silence before Ellison's mother burst into laughter. "I'm—I'm sorry, love, he's fourteen," she giggled, covering her mouth. "I think he's looking for something a little more practical."

Papa smiled. "Well then, fine. Your mother says my advice is no good, Ellison," he teased, nudging her. "Let's see what she has to say!"

Mum placed her book on her lap and sat up. "What your father means is that the entire point of the Trace System is to achieve the True Victory. To follow your Trace so well that upon death, you replace your Trace's Celestim."

"We talked about that earlier today," Papa told her.

Ellison nodded. In a flash, he remembered the awkward conversation with his father and Gwen earlier that day. He wanted to ask about it, to know what had pushed Papa far enough to snap like that, but he didn't know how to bring it up gently.

"So," Mum continued, "If you want the best possible chance of achieving the True Victory, which Trace should you choose?" At his lingering confusion, she began again. "If you had to look at yourself *now*, which of the Traces would you say best represents you?"

Ellison sighed. "I'm not sure, then. Maybe...Humility?"

His mother frowned. "I don't think so, dear. Just—just keep thinking. You'll find it eventually, and when you do, you'll know."

She seemed to think that this was the end of the conversation because at this point, she set her book on her nightstand and extinguished the candle next to it. "Good night, my boys."

"Good night, Mum," Ell sighed.

He thought for a few more minutes before deciding that he'd come to no clear decision tonight. Pulling his blanket up to his chin, he tipped his mind into the place of heroes and fantasies. The place where he was a hero.

Chapter 4
Lord Blackworth, pt. II

"Hold fast, men!" he cried.

Arrows and boulders flew as the enemy forces flung projectiles at the city walls. Even now, upon the ramparts, an arrow shot towards Blackworth's face, and he barely raised the flat of his blade in time to deflect it.

It had been three weeks since Lord Blackworth had retaken his home. Gripper's men had returned to their land and told the emperor of their defeat. The enemy leader had rapidly launched a counterattack, and now Blackworth was defending his home from atop the city walls.

"My lord, what will we do?" asked Alistair, standing behind him.

"I must protect my people," he replied. "Alistair, stay here. I'm going down."

"Down where?"

"Onto the fields!" he called, stepping up to the wall's edge. "Look, Alistair! There's no infantry down there, only archers. They won't stand a chance!" He glanced at the ground below, roughly forty hands down.

"But my lord—"

Without another word, Blackworth leapt off the ramparts.

The fall was instantaneous, and he rolled to a stop. As Blackworth hit the ground, he could hear his men crying out in alarm from atop the wall.

On the field before him were hordes of soldiers with shortbows drawn. A few of the quicker ones dropped their bows and reached for hand axes or short swords, but the vast majority just froze. Blackworth shifted his blade in hand and charged.

The enemy archers had no chance against his speed. His blade sliced through their armor with ease, and not one of their pitiful attacks came close.

For the first few minutes, he was more of a butcher than a soldier, cutting them down with no actual resistance. It was only after he'd slaughtered about fifteen or so of them down that the first counterattack came. He batted the enemy's blade away easily and backhanded the man who'd swung it with his thick metal gauntlet.

Blackworth lost track of time. It could've been hours, it could've been just a few minutes. But soon, the attacking soldiers regained their wits and began to circle him.

He came to life, his longsword an extension of his arm. There was no thinking, no tactical moves. Instinct was what kept Blackworth alive now. Luckily, he had plenty. As some children were raised to be musicians or scholars, Blackworth had been raised a warrior. To wield a blade was as natural as speaking.

Within minutes, his hair was soaked with blood and sweat, his face painted scarlet. Blackworth's grip on his sword was slick with viscera. He ducked an attack and thrust his blade into an attacker's chest. As he wrenched his sword back, the handle slipped. The sword was lodged in the enemy archer's chest, leaving Blackworth unarmed.

His blade gone, he fought with renewed fury. He struck with fists and boots, deflecting attacks on his bracers of gleaming steel. But he was tiring, and he had no assistance.

One of the attackers kicked at the inside of his knee from behind and Blackworth was flung to the ground. He tried to stand, but the attacks were coming from all sides—he was barely able to defend himself.

In a flash, a brilliant arc of light cut through one of the men from behind. There, to the left—it cut through another, and another. The enemies, one by one, turned their attention from Blackworth to this new assailant.

She broke through the ranks until she was right next to him. Brilliant pale hair glowing in the sunlight, her skin was flecked with blood, her white armor stark against the dark leather of the enemy soldiers. "Alistair said you came down by yourself!" she cried.

Blackworth shrugged, ducking an attack. "I had it under control."

She laughed. "I'm sure you did, love. Now, would you mind joining me?" In one fluid motion, she drew his blade from the corpse it had lodged itself in and tossed it his way. Blackworth caught his sword and—

"Ellison!"

Firion Crippled, I swear—

It was Gwen's voice, that was sure. But what she was doing in his parents' room, in the middle of the night, Ellison had no idea. "Wake up, Ell! Come on, *wake up!*"

"What?" Ellison hissed, sitting up. "What do you want, Gwenli?" As he sat forward, he collided with her face.

"Oh—ow," she groaned, rubbing her nose.

"What is it, Gwen?"

"Ow…ugh." She ran a hand through her blonde hair, eyes sparkling with excitement in the dim light. "Ell, there's something you have to see!"

"Gwenli…" he paused. "Did you sneak out? Your parents said—"

24

"They won't know," Gwen whispered. "We'll be back in ten minutes. Come on, Ell. If we wait, they'll be gone!"

"What does *that* mean?"

"Oh, come on," she sighed, pausing for his response. "Come on!"

Ellison took a deep breath and stood. "Fine," he grumbled, grabbing his own cloak from its spot on the floor. "This better be worth it."

Chapter 5
Darkness

Ellison sucked in a breath as he followed Gwenli out the tavern's back door into the cold night air. "How far is it?" he whispered. "And *what* is it?"

"Not too far," she muttered distractedly.

He could hear the lie in her voice, but he followed anyway. Ell had been friends with Gwen long enough to know that when she wanted to show him something, it was usually worth seeing.

Gwenli led him down the quiet cobblestone street with the confidence of an aristocrat. Ellison didn't think he'd taken a single step in his life with that same sureness—he almost envied it.

After a few seconds, she led him down a smaller side-street, this one paved with gravel. The oil-lamps that burned every few paces down the street didn't follow into this less-trafficked alley, and quickly, the two children were submerged in darkness. "Gwen, are you sure we're supposed to be out?"

She laughed. "Of course not, that's half the fun."

"I think we have different definitions of fun," Ellison whispered. He felt his stomach constrict as every scary story his mother had ever told him about wandering through the city came flooding back. Gwen's pace was rushed, and Ellison had to walk fast to keep up with her. Quickly, they were out on a main street again, and the streetlamps brought at least the illusion of safety. There were beggars on some of the street-corners, sleeping or just sitting, counting the coins they had earned in daylight. Their wild eyes and shaky hands twisted Ellison's stomach further, and the sound of the loose coins in his cloak pocket became overloud in his ears. "Where are we going? You said it wasn't far!"

She shrugged. "It wasn't. They must've kept walking."

"What?" he hissed. "Who are you talking about?"

Gwen paused in her tracks. "Do you want to know now, or do you want it to be a surprise?"

It was a good thing it was dark, because otherwise she'd have seen the look of shock and frustration on Ell's face. "Tell me now!" he cried. "What made you think I wanted it to be a surprise?"

She sighed. "Okay, okay, calm down. Here it is, then. Er—actually, we should keep walking. Come on." Again, Gwenli set off down the path, Ellison at her side.

"What are we walking towards, Gwen?"

"Monarchs," she hummed, the smile evident in her voice.

"What?" he frowned. "The Monarchs? Like…the Monarchs?"

She giggled. "Of course, like *the Monarchs*. I was walking and I just saw 'em. Two of 'em, walking side by side. They were going this way, giving money and food to beggars. Now come on!"

The Monarchs were the most powerful people in Caraspen. The rulers, the heads of state, the…the monarchs. There were four of them—Kaene, Prime Chancellor, Sovereign, and Surveyor. They lived in Castle Firalos, the great castle at the center of Aelos itself. From Firalos, they led the entire nation. They were powerful, wealthy, famous—the kings and queens over Caraspen.

Ellison blinked. "Are you joking with me, Gwen? Be serious."

"Oh, I saw them. Problem is," she peered around a street corner, "I can't find them again."

"Are you...wait, Gwenli, are we lost?"

She didn't answer.

"Firion Crippled!" Ellison burst, the panic immediately taking hold. "You don't know where we are?"

"I suppose...I could probably find our way back, if..." she sighed. "Okay, yes. We're lost."

We're going to die. Why did I let her do this? Why did I trust her? he thought. *Stupid, Ellison. How are you going to get home now? You should've paid more attention, now what?*

"Hee-hee, hee-hee..."

Ellison tensed, spinning to the source of the sound. All he could see was a shadowed figure at the end of the alley, behind them. "Ell," Gwen whispered, "what is that?"

Another high peal of laughter rang out from down the street.

The shadow was growing larger.

He opened his mouth, but no words came out. At that moment, Ellison became aware of just how dark it was, and just how unarmed he and Gwenli were. *We're going to die.*

"You know," Gwen began muttering to herself, "perhaps we should turn back. They probably weren't the Monarchs anyway, they were probably just two rich people. I didn't really see them clearly, it was dark..."

"What are you two doing out here?"

It was a cold, slick voice. Unhinged. Chaotic, otherworldly. Terrifying.

We're going to die.

"Did you hear that?" Gwen mouthed.

28

Mum always said Gwen would be the death of me. I guess she was right.

"Are you lost?" the voice called. A man's voice, like ice down Ellison's back.

"Ell," Gwenli whispered, her voice shaking.

"Who—who's there?" he called, suddenly aware of how immature his voice sounded in his own ears.

Gwen tugged him along, but Ellison was frozen in his tracks. The fear had taken him over. He couldn't move. "Ell?" she whispered. "Come on!"

"It's not wise for young children like yourselves to be out so late," the voice drawled, closer now. "What are your names?"

"Ell, we have to run," Gwenli hissed, pulling frantically at his wrist.

He'd been warned too many times of dangerous men prowling through city streets at night. Slavers, his mother said.

"He—he's coming, he's…"

"Where are you off to, children?"

Slaver.

"Come *on*," she growled, jerking him forward. Finally, Ellison snapped from his daze and started running. Fast. Towards light, towards maybe another person to help them, or even just somewhere to hide. He ran, Gwenli behind him. His only thought was putting the next foot down faster than the one before.

Ellison could hear the man running after them. *What does he want with us?*

"Don't run!" the man cried, laughing as he ran. "I don't want to hurt you! What are your names?"

Suddenly, Gwen tripped on a loose chunk of gravel and rolled to the ground. Ellison came to a stop and turned to help her up, the man's feet still audible from the shadows.

"I'm coming, I'm coming!" he called, a peal of manic laughter escaping his lips. "I'm coming! You'd better run!"

What does he want with us—

Gwenli scrambled to her feet, and together, they tore off again. But they weren't fast enough. The man was right behind them, his breath on their necks, reaching out.

All of a sudden, Ell felt a heavy force slam into him from behind. He went sprawling onto the cobblestones, rolling across the street. The wind was driven from his lungs.

"Ellison!" Gwenli cried as he came to a stop on his stomach. "Ell, help, he's—"

Ellison looked up at Gwen.

The man had caught her.

"Ellison, help me!"

His eyes stood out in the shadows of his hood—the darkness played tricks and made them look almost red. The skin of his bare hands was ice-pale. He had a fist around the collar of Gwenli's dress. "Hello, darling."

"Ellison!"

But he didn't move. The fear was crippling.

He'll kill me. I'm just a boy, I can't stop a grown man.

"Ellison, please!" Gwen's voice was desperate, terrified.

Save yourself, Ellison, said a voice in his head. *You'll die if you try to save her.*

He could've gotten up. But he didn't.

What are you doing? he thought.

I…I can't do it, a voice answered.

He was no hero. He was not like the legendary warriors of old. He was not Lord Blackworth. He was just a boy, too scared to save his friend.

The man's laughter rang through the night air. Ellison watched as the man began to pull Gwenli backwards into the night shadows.

I could run after her, he knew. *He's not far enough away yet that I can't catch him. I could do it.*

He stayed still.

She will be sold into slavery.

He gave up.

There's no use trying—

BOOM!

Impossible heat blasted past Ellison's face. Brilliant purple light flashed up in his face and he fell to the ground.

He heard Gwenli cry out from down the alley. The light had seared his vision, he couldn't see anything.

Something grabbed him by his forearm. Ell jerked against the arm and flailed his arms out in panic.

A hand deflected his punch almost gently. "Woah there, son! Easy!"

It wasn't the man's voice—it was someone else. "Go back to the shadows, thief!" A woman's voice. As Ellison's vision began to return, he saw a fair lady standing over him, her arm outstretched towards their silk-voiced attacker.

"What in Rahthe's burning breath—" Ellison started, trying again to break the woman's grip. But she was strong, and he had no chance. "Gwen?" he screamed.

Another voice, a third, cut through the night. Another man. It sounded like a storm, like a tree falling. "Flee this place," he shouted past Ellison. "Leave them alone!"

Standing there amidst the shadows was the attacker, near-invisible in the darkness. In fact, Ellison wouldn't have known he was there if it wasn't for the fact that his clothes were half-consumed with purple fire. Gwen was frantically scrambling down the alley towards them.

The next thing to happen was fast. From the woman's outstretched palm, a jet of violet purple fire— hot, blazing, bright—burst forth like a javelin and spiraled toward the shadowed man.

31

The man dove to the side, the flame bolt missing by just a breath. His features were blurred by the flickering shadows, but Ellison could make out a look of pleasure in his face. Even half-aflame, he looked almost…satisfied? There was a semi-permanent smirk at the corner of his lips, and his eyes were dancing with amusement.

As Ell watched, the third voice—the one who had commanded the attacker to leave—stepped into view. It was a man in regal clothing, wearing a brilliant blue cloak. He had one arm around Gwen, who was scraped up quite badly. "Leave, I said! Go!"

The attacker stood, patting the flames out of his robe. His face was pale, his eyes almost red in the firelight. He gave a quick smile—the kind meant to put you at ease. Ellison only felt more terrified than before. "Fine."

As he turned to leave, he winked. Right at Ellison.

Then, he turned on his heel and ran off back down the alley. In seconds, the man was gone. At the same second, Gwen collapsed into Ellison's arms, and he slid back against the wall, breathing shakily. She sobbed into his shoulder, and he fought back tears of his own. *Oh, Firion. I…oh, Firion Crippled.*

"Are you two alright?" the man asked.

I gave up on her. She trusted me. Ellison felt like throwing up.

The woman extinguished the flame in her palm. "Sorry, love. I didn't mean to hurt you. I just didn't want you going after him."

I wasn't going to go after him, he thought. *I was going to let Gwen be taken because I was scared.* He was a fraud. He was a coward. *She could've been murdered, raped, or sold into slavery.*

Gwen turned and looked up at them, blinking through tear-blurred eyes. "Who are you?"

"I'm Isra," the woman replied, "And this is Anroth."

Ellison stared, dumb, at the man and woman who had saved their lives. Only now was he able to get a thorough look at them. The woman wore a forest-green dress, her dark hair in a single plaited braid. The man wore a blue cloak, as he'd noticed, along with fine grey tunic and trousers. He reached into his cloak and produced a vial of something. Ellison couldn't see what it was but watched as the man turned his back and fiddled with it.

Anroth turned back to them. "May I take your hand, etsa?" he asked Gwen, still huddled against Ellison. She stared hesitantly at him and made no move.

"Please, etsa," the man whispered. He used the female honorific 'etsa' when addressing Gwen, similar to 'madame' or 'my lady.' "I'm only trying to help you. I can take care of your scrapes."

Gwen slowly stood up and held her arm out.

Anroth smiled and stepped forward. "Thank you." He took her hand in his own and closed his eyes.

In a flash, Gwenli cried aloud and drew her arm back. "What in Rahthe's burning breath was that?"

Anroth smirked to Isra, who slapped him on the arm. "Don't tease the poor girl," she sighed, then turning to Gwen, said, "Look at your knees, love."

"It *hurt*," she hissed, almost breaking into sobs again.

"I'm sorry it hurt, but it helped you, I promise," said Anroth. "Trust me, just look."

Gwen tugged her pants up above her knees and looked down. "How did you do that?"

Ellison stepped around her so he could see what she saw. Her legs, her knees…they were healed. Perfectly whole again. The blood from the scrapes was still there but the wounds themselves were knit back together.

"Magic," Anroth smiled, "or science, depending on your understanding. It's called Hemosia."

Ellison turned the word over in his mouth like a seashell between his fingers. "Who are you?" He had

33

scrapes of his own, but he didn't mention them. Gwen's wounds were those of a true victim. Ellison deserved to keep his for longer. A badge of shame.

"We told you our names already," the woman smiled.

The man—Anroth—laughed. "Come, Isradellar. Don't be facetious."

"I'm not," she frowned.

How did you make that man run off?" Gwenli asked, her voice still wavering. Ellison only now realized that her fingers were locked in his and wondered how long they'd been like that.

"Another kind of magic," Isra answered. "Caustisia."

"How did you learn it, koso?" Gwenli murmured.

Again, Anroth laughed. "Well, yes…sorry. I can't do it any longer. You two aren't native to Aelos, are you?"

The children both shook their heads.

"That explains it, then," he said. "My apologies. Of course, you wouldn't recognize us."

"What do you mean?"

"Allow us to introduce ourselves," said Anroth. "Properly, this time. I am Anroth Ularael, Sovereign of Caraspen."

"And I am Isradellar Yesdas, Kaene of Caraspen," said Isra, bowing gently. "But please, just call me Isra."

Gwen squeaked. Ellison suddenly became aware of his shabby, tattered cloak and tousled bed-hair. "Er, you're…"

"Monarchs, yes," Isra finished. "Well, two out of the four. Now, can we take you two home?"

Chapter 6
Isra and Anroth

Ellison remembered the name of the tavern from when his father had told him earlier that day and relayed it to the Monarchs. Isra stayed with the children for a few minutes as Anroth walked off looking for directions. When he came back, the four of them set off.

The Monarchs tried to make conversation, but both children were too dumbstruck to do anything except nod or shake their heads. Anroth and Isra picked up on their fright and began conversing privately. This left Ell and Gwen some privacy of their own, and for the first time, Ellison looked to his best friend while they walked.

"Are you alright?" he asked.

She nodded and took a deep breath, brushing a hair out of her face. "I'm fine. Just a little shaken up."

"I'm so sorry," he whispered.

"For what?"

"I—" he paused. "He almost took you."

"That's not your fault," she said.

She didn't understand.

Perhaps it was better that way.

"Who—who do you think that man was?" Gwen eventually said.

"A thief, or a slaver," he murmured. "A bad man."

"No," she sighed. "He was more than that."

"What do you mean?"

"The Kaene set him on *fire*, Ellison, and he didn't care. That's more than just a regular man…isn't it?" Gwen's eyes were as glassy as his had been before.

"He…he winked," Ell whispered.

"What?"

"Before he ran off, he winked at me. I didn't remember until just now." The image haunted him.

"I…I'm sorry," she murmured. "I shouldn't have led you—this is all my fault."

"No, it—" he paused. But how could he explain what he was thinking? She wouldn't understand. "It's okay, Gwen."

She frowned. "Ellison, I almost got us killed. Please, you're allowed to hate me."

"I don't hate you," he said. "Why would you think that?"

Gwen sighed. "I don't know."

"I could never hate you," he added after a moment.

"Why not?"

Ellison looked away. "I don't know," he shrugged. And that was the truth.

The conversation quieted, and in the silence, Ellison again remembered the man. *Who was he? Why did he want us?*

It just didn't make sense. The man had done too many peculiar things to just be another street-thief. There was the look of amusement on his face and the manic laughter in his voice, but there was also the red glare in his eyes, the way he'd barely cared that Isra had set him afire. The way he'd winked.

He resolved to find out one day. Perhaps not today, nor even in the next year. But before he died, he would learn who that man was, and why he'd winked.

They tried convincing the Monarchs to just let them go up into the tavern by themselves, but Anroth and Isra were set on making sure Ellison and Gwenli were safe with their parents before they left. "Young etsa has a tear in her pants," Anroth explained. Indeed, Ellison saw a rip as long as his hand in the side of Gwen's trousers. "We'd be amiss if we didn't leave a bit of coin for her parents to buy her a new pair."

"No, no," Gwen whispered as they entered the tavern. "I'll just stitch it up before I go to bed, it's no problem. Please, thank you so much, but—"

"Nonsense, love," Isra insisted. "We really don't mind."

Ellison felt his stomach sinking. The only thing scarier than the dark attacker was the idea of what his father would do if he discovered his son had snuck out at night. "Please, we don't mean to offend," he said. "It's just that—"

Suddenly, a figure approached from behind the bar. The tavernkeeper, dark circles around his eyes. " 'scuse me," he muttered. "We don't take customers a'…whatever the hell time it is. Come back—oh." His eyes widened and he stumbled back a few paces, obviously recognizing Isra and Anroth. "Oh, my breathing days. Lord koso, Lady etsa, I'm so sorry. My deepest apologies." 'Koso' was the male equivalent of 'etsa', the honorific Anroth had used when addressing Gwen earlier.

"It's alright, my friend," said Anroth. "We're simply returning these two to their parents. I believe they have rooms at your establishment."

"Yes, koso," the man bowed again. "Er—children, what rooms are your parents in?"

Gwen relayed the numbers quietly.

The tavernkeeper sighed and disappeared into a back room. While they waited, Isra turned to Ell and Gwenli and smiled. "I...I don't believe I ever asked you two your names."

"This is Gwenli, and I'm Ellison," he answered. "Blackworth, that is."

"Brother and sister?" Isra asked.

Gwenli wrinkled her nose. "No, definitely not. Just friends." Wordless, she slipped her hand out of Ellison's for the first time since they'd met the Monarchs.

After a few minutes, the sound of footsteps was heard from the staircase. Again, Ell's stomach twisted. *Papa,* he thought.

Indeed, his father was quickly visible in the dim light of the empty taproom, standing on the landing of the staircase. His eyes were bleary, but his posture was alert. Behind him came Gwenli's parents and Ell's mum behind them.

"Ellison!" Papa hissed, moving forward towards him. "What are you—"

"You must be the parents of these two," Isra smiled, interrupting him with a short bow.

"Er—yes," Papa began. He didn't recognize her as the barkeeper had. "I'm sorry—what have they done? We can pay for whatever—"

"No, no," Isra explained. "They haven't done anything wrong. We simply wanted to make certain that they were in safe hands before we let them out of our sight."

"These two had a run-in with an unpleasant sort of fellow," Anroth said. "Don't worry, it's no sort of law trouble. Let's just say it's a good thing we were able to step in."

"Are you hurt, you two?" asked Mum, following Gwen's father closer. When she saw Gwenli's bloody pants, she put a hand to her mouth. "What happened?"

"It's nothing, Mum," Gwen promised. "We're okay."

"Well, they're alright now," Gwen's father murmured, stepping off the stairs into the light. "You may—oh. Oh, my lord and lady." He bowed to the waist. "I—I had no idea, we…"

"Ah, drast," Isra swore. "I thought you weren't Aelosi?"

"What do you mean?" Papa frowned. "We're caravanners. Why does it matter—" Ellison watched as his father took a moment to recognize the Monarchs and gasped. As he spoke, he stepped closer into the light. "Oh, my apologies. I didn't know, I—" he bowed. "If I'd known I was speaking with the Sovereign, I—and the children, they weren't supposed to be out. We've told them before—"

"It's alright, koso," Isra shrugged. "There's no need to apologize. But we'd better be on our way back to the castle." She turned to Ellison and Gwenli. *They mean Castle Firalos,* Ell realized distantly. "You two, be careful in cities like this. There won't always be someone nearby to protect you. Next time, you might have to save yourselves."

"Next time…" Mum whispered. "What happened?"

"They'll explain it all, I'm sure," said Anroth as he and Isra began walking towards the door. "Goodnight, children. It was a pleasure meeting you. Stay safe!"

And with that, the Monarchs popped out the door and were gone, leaving Ellison and Gwenli alone in the dark taproom with their parents.

There was silence for half a minute while the children and their parents processed everything that had just happened.

"Alright, you two," Gwenli's father said. "Sit down and explain yourselves."

The next day was sell-day as planned, but Ellison wasn't a third trader with his mother and father. Instead, he sat in the back of the wagon from sunrise to sunset, shelling the sipa nuts they'd collected outside of the city a few days back. By noon, his fingers ached from the work, and when Papa finally said he could stop, it was time to head back to the tavern.

Gwen had it worse. Her mother gave her the job of record-keeper. It was her duty, from the start to end of the workday, to record every sale made by every wagon in the caravan. She spent the entire time running to and fro through the market square, scribbling on a ledger. Every time Ellison's parents signaled her over to note a sale, Ell gave her a quick glance and went back to shelling his sipa nuts. He didn't get to talk to her all day, not until dinner, when all the other children went out to see the travelling performers at the street corner. Their parents made them both stay inside and help the tavernkeeper with dishes until after the show was finished.

The punishments Ellison and Gwenli received on sell-day were harsh, but the morning after that, their parents began to lessen the severity of their punishments. As they began to pack up their things and get the wagons ready to travel, Ellison got to work shelling sipa nuts again. After an hour, Papa barked for him to put the work down and go with Grandpa Emory to pay the tavernkeeper. When he came back, the nuts were put away, and nothing more was said of it.

He couldn't shake the guilt. The memory of lying there while the man pulled Gwen backwards into the darkness…the high laughter clashing with her screams…he couldn't stop thinking about it.

He tried to find solace in daydreams, but even that didn't work. He could never go back to Lord Blackworth—he couldn't pretend he was a hero, now that he knew the truth. Now that he knew that when the moment came for him to do the right thing, he had failed.

The loudest voice in my ears was the one between them, he thought. *Like Papa said. I let the voice in my head beat me.*

I will not let myself be beaten by my own fears again. Never. I will not fail Gwen, or anyone, like that ever again.

By the third day, they'd left Aelos behind and with it their punishment. Ell's thoughts once again drifted to the impossibility of choosing a Trace, but every now and then, he remembered the man, the attacker. The dark-robed figure who caught fire, laughed, and ran off.

Chapter 7
Grandpa and Grandma

On their first day out of Aelos, the wagons were rolling a little lighter. The caravanners walked with heavier pockets and bigger smiles than before. Winter was approaching, and the past few days' profits would ensure them warmth and comfort when they reached their next destination.

The next stop would come in about three weeks. There, they'd use the profits from Aelos to buy rare goods from across the sea and within the city. Then it was on to the next stop, where they'd sell the wares and repeat the process.

While the caravan rolled along with Ellison's father at the front, Ell himself wandered the line. Gwen was helping her mother give some of the younger girls a lesson in sewing patches, so he was idle for company.

Luckily, he found someone to talk to rather quickly. Grandpa Emory walked beside the third wagon in the line. That's where Grandma Elise rode, and Grandpa Emory liked to keep her company.

"Hey there, boy!" his grandfather smiled as Ellison caught up to where Grandpa Em was walking. Grandma Elise sat on the ledge of the wagon, chatting with his grandfather.

Technically speaking, Grandma Elise Lovedale was not Ellison's grandmother—in fact, she was Gwen's. The Lovedale family, along with the Blackworth family, had been members of the troupe for generations. Grandma Elise had, for as long as Ellison could remember, professed to being 'everyone's grandmother', and so whether they were related by blood or not, every child in the caravan referred to her as such. She and Grandpa Em weren't married, but they were the only two of their generation still with the caravan. As such, they spent most days together, bickering or telling old stories.

"Good morning, koso," Ellison nodded. "How's your knee today?" Grandpa Emory suffered from what he called a 'gimp limb' and Mum called arthritis in his left knee.

"Drast the thing, boy!" the old man cried. "It's a beautiful day, and by Firion's Crippled body, a rotted knee isn't going to stop me from enjoying it."

Grandma Elise clicked her tongue. "Watch your language, Emory Blackworth."

"I'll do as I please, Elise Lovedale," he smiled. "Unless my mother has been reborn in your old body, I will kindly decline your chidings on my speech."

"Kindly?" she frowned. "I see nothing kind about it, disrespecting an old woman so…"

"Oh, drast an 'old woman!' " he snapped. "That won't work on me, you know. I'm older than you." He grumbled something under his breath, then turned to Ellison. "I'm sure you didn't come over here to listen to our geriatric bickering. What are you thinking about today?"

Ell paused. There was no use dodging the truth—Grandpa Em and Grandma Elise would know the truth eventually. "My Trace Declaration is two prayers away, and—"

"A-ha!" Grandpa Em chuckled, poking a finger at Elise. "I told you he'd come!"

"What?" Ellison frowned, flushing.

Grandma Elise scowled. "He was telling me a few days back that you'd be around to ask for advice on picking your Trace. You know I *agreed* with you, Emory. You didn't win anything."

"Oh, bother. Well, Ellison, we'll tell you what we told Gwenli. It's not—"

"You spoke to Gwen?" said Ellison.

"Oh, yes," Grandma Elise smiled. "She came to us both about a prayer back. Why, did she not tell you?"

"Firion Crippled and all the Celestim in the sky," Grandpa Em snapped, "did his reaction not spell that out clearly enough?"

"My breathing *days*, I swear that's enough of your picking for today, Emory Blackworth."

Grandpa Em chuckled, slipping his hands into his pockets.

"Now, honey, what are you worried about?"

Ellison paused, then said, "It's just that...I don't know what to do. I don't know what I'm going to choose or how to even go about making a choice. Please, don't tell my Mum and Papa," he added after a moment. "I don't want them to know."

"Of course not," Grandma Elise smiled. "Trace Declarations are decisions, great decisions. And everywhere there's a decision, there's fear."

"Fear of what?"

"Fear of making the wrong choice," she explained. "You don't want to pick a Trace that you might regret. Am I right?"

Ellison nodded.

"You aren't the only person who's ever felt this way," she said. "Thousands, even millions of people, over the years, have panicked about their Trace Declaration. You aren't alone. And yes, some are blessed with self-knowledge from a young age." Ellison thought of Gwen, already so sure of her choice. He wondered if she'd been that sure before talking to Grandpa Em and Grandma Elise. "But the majority of us, at age fourteen, aren't done becoming ourselves yet. And that scares us. What if I choose Humility and realize that I have a deep-rooted problem with arrogance? What if I choose Ambition and realize that I'm simply not ambitious enough to sustain a lifetime of that?"

Ellison nodded again. "So how do I get around it? How do I make a choice?"

"Well," said Grandpa Emory, "I don't have perfect advice for you. I can't tell you that you'll make the perfect decision. But that's because there's simply no such thing."

"What do you mean?"

"The perfect Trace, the perfect decision does not exist," his grandfather explained. "No person is completely Brave or Curious or Loving. We're all a cluster of emotions and desires and logics. But that's okay. The point of the Trace System isn't to pick the one that you most closely align with."

"It's...it's not?"

"Of course not!" Grandpa Em laughed. "Just look at Grandma Elise. She might Trace Joy, but I can tell you firsthand—"

"Are you sure you'd like to go that route, Emory?" she interrupted. "Nobody in their right mind would be less than shocked when they learned you Trace Chivalry—at least, not anyone who's ever seen you speak to your betters."

"My betters? I hope you don't mean yourself," he shot back, winking at Ellison.

"Oh, never mind," sighed Grandma Elise. "Ellison, the point of the Trace System is to pick the one that you most closely *want to* align with. Not one that you think you already do align with. Understand the difference?"

Grandpa Em started. "Here—let me explain. When you're up there on the stage in front of everyone, you aren't meant to say 'I'm Tracing Peace because I think I am a very peaceful boy.' Rahthe's burning breath, no wonder you were so worried! If that were the goal, nobody would be able to even come close to picking a Trace.

"My boy, here's what it's about. When you stand before us all, before your community and your Celestial Chorus above, we're watching not for what you think you match best. Nobody could pick that at so young an age."

"Look at the spread," Grandma Elise explained, "the list of Traces. You pick the one that you want to match best. For me, as a little girl, that was Joy. So I declared Joy and devoted my life to trying to be Joyous. Emory Blackworth, don't even start. No, I wasn't *perfect* at it, and there were times I wasn't even close. But I tried, and I feel better for trying. Now, do you have something in mind?"

No, he thought. *But I suppose it's a start.*

Chapter 8
Declaration

The day came quickly—and rather rudely, Ellison thought. One morning it was there, and he still hadn't made a decision.

Now, Ellison sat alone on a log. At sundown, he and Gwenli would announce their Traces to the caravan.

His hands shook. In less than an hour, he would stand before the men, women, and children he'd grown up around, and would announce the Trace he'd follow for the rest of his life.

They'd set up camp around lunchtime in order to have time to prepare for the Declarations. In the nearby clearing, Ellison watched as the ceremony's preparations took place. A large fire was lit in the center and a few wagons drawn together, the tops removed, to act as a stage.

A stage he would soon find himself upon.

Hours later, Ellison stood behind the platform, tucked in shadow. All eyes were on Gwenli, who stood atop the stage, illuminated by the blazing fire below her. On the other side of the flames stood the caravanners.

"I, Gwenli Asfina, daughter of Derros and Safsario Asfina, hereby declare that I will, to the best of my ability and to the end of my days, Trace Curiosity."

A breath. Silence...applause. The crackle of the fire was drowned out by the clapping and cheering of the small crowd. Gwenli hastily hopped off of the platform and ran to where her mother and father awaited with open arms. Ellison's parents stood next to them, his mother chewing her lip.

Oh, Firion, God Above All, Ellison prayed, *help me. Please, don't let me make the wrong choice.*

As the applause died, all eyes shifted back to the stage. Ellison felt sick.

He stepped slowly towards the platform.

"Um, hello....my name—er, you know my name, I'm—I am Ellison Blackworth, son of Hanik and Issela Blackworth. I—well—I hereby declare that I will, to the best of my ability and to the end of my days, Trace..." He paused and looked out over the crowd. His mother and father stood arm in arm, Mum gnawing her lip anxiously and Papa rocking back and forth. Near them stood Grandma Elise and Grandpa Emory, who gave Ell a wink and a nod. *It's not what you* are, the old man mouthed.

It's what you want, Ell thought. *What do I want?*

He thought back to that night with Gwen in Aelos. How he'd given up on her, how he'd failed his best friend. How he'd resolved never to let that happen again.

And, suddenly, his choice was clear.

"Right," Ellison began. "I will, to the best of my ability and to the end of days, Trace Perseverance."

The next few moments passed in a haze. Afterwards, when he looked back on the night, he had no recollection of stepping off of the platform. He must have, though, because the next thing he knew, Ell was in his mother's arms.

"Congratulations! You did it! Oh, congratulations!" she exclaimed, jumping up and down. "Perseverance!"

His father stood next to her, beaming just as wide. "I'll be honest, son…I wasn't sure you were going to say *anything* there for a moment. You looked like you were about to run off the stage!"

"Oh hush, Hanik!" said Mum. "He did a fantastic job! Beautiful, really, love."

Ellison flushed but didn't know what to say. He didn't want to admit how close to the truth his father had been, so he just laughed and gave him a hug.

"Th—thank you, Mum," he replied. "Grandpa Em—"

Before he could finish his statement, something—or someone—crashed into him, nearly toppling him over. Ell spun and found his best friend, steadying herself on Papa.

"Sorry, pa," she apologized before turning to embrace Ellison. "Congratulations!" Gwenli's eyes glittered and sparkled with excitement.

He laughed. "Congratulations to you, too! You didn't seem nervous at all!"

From amidst the crowd, a fiddle struck up a lively tune. His parents left Ellison and Gwenli, joining hands to dance with the rest of the caravan. Their caravan didn't often shy away from an opportunity to celebrate.

After watching the dancing for a moment, Ellison turned back to Gwen. She stood, her face flickering with shadows from the bonfire nearby. "Perseverance," she smiled. "Why…why, if I can ask, Perseverance?"

"Grandpa Em and Grandma Elise told me to choose the Trace I want to be, not the Trace I am. I wasn't exactly sure what that was until…well, until I was up on that stage."

Gwen laughed. "Your voice is still shaking."

"I was so scared!" Ell ran a hand through his hair. "That was terrifying."

Gwenli nodded, her eyes alight. "Me too. I was so worried I'd forget the right words."

She smiled again, and all of a sudden, something changed for Ellison. It might've been the adrenaline or perhaps the way the firelight reflected off of her skin, but he suddenly became aware of how close Gwenli was standing. A dozen thoughts ran through his mind all at once.

She's always stood this close to me, hasn't she? This isn't odd. But why does it feel different? She's so...

She smells nice.

Her eyes...I never noticed her eyes like that. Hmm.

And in that single moment, Ellison's view of Gwenli changed. Everything became different.

She's...beautiful.

It was like he'd never seen her before now. Yes, he'd looked at her, but he hadn't *seen* her. At least not in this way. *But how?* he wondered. *How had I not noticed this before now? And why do I finally see it now? She's just...Gwen.*

Trace Declarations were a big part of Aesekri peoples' lives, and they had concrete cultural impact. It was Caraspeni tradition for girls to wear their hair in two braids until they declared their Trace, and then, after they made their Declaration, their mother would tie their hair into a single braid. That was how they wore it, traditionally, until marriage.

Ell hadn't noticed, but Gwen's hair was in a single braid. All his life, she'd worn it in two frizzy blonde braids. Now, for the first time, she looked different. Gwenli wore her single braid with maturity, age, and...beauty. *It's gorgeous,* Ell thought.

Only now did he realize just how long he had been staring at her. Gwen flushed and smiled, staring down at her feet. A half-giggle escaped her lips, and Ellison felt his mouth dry up.

Yes, he was certain now. She was beautiful. Her green eyes and her newly braided blonde hair, it was the loveliest thing he'd ever seen. The dress she wore barely brushed her ankles, and Ellison glanced down at the belt around her waist. He was suddenly thinking things he'd never, ever thought before.

Suddenly, Gwen grabbed his hand. "Would you like to dance?"

Ellison nodded as quickly as he could.

"Good," she laughed, tugging him towards the music.

Chapter 9
Gwenli, pt. II

Dearest Grist, Celestim of Perseverance, thank you for blessing my family and myself.

Ellison sat against a tree, his eyes closed, the bottom of his pants wet with morning dew. Grandpa Em and Mum sat nearby in their own secluded places.

It was the morning of his first prayer. Before, he'd always just slept in with the rest of the children or talked to Gwen until the adults finished their prayers, but now he had a Trace. While the rest of the little ones slept, Mum had shaken Ellison awake and led him off into a private place for his first prayer.

He'd memorized the beginning easily enough. Now came the hard part. Each Celestim had a name—Submission, the leader of the Nirrin, had been Rahthe. Perseverance's name was Grist. Grandma Elise said it was easier to pray to someone called Grist than to Perseverance, and Ell agreed. She'd said to speak like he was speaking to a friend. There was no need for fancy speech—the Celestim understood all kinds of talk.

Lord Grist...I have never done this before. Well, I suppose you knew that. Papa says the Celestim know everything that happens.

I wonder why I still have to pray, if that's so. Don't you already know what I'm going to say?

He paused, and after remembering he wasn't going to get answer, began again.

I wonder who else is praying to you right now. There must be hundreds, at least. Hundreds of other people Tracing Perseverance at the same time as me, hundreds trying to do a better job than me at pushing forward through adversity.

I've heard of other religions that believe different sorts of things about prayer. Some even say they can pray at any moment of the day and their god will hear them. I suppose that would be nice.

Again, he paused as if expecting a reply. When none came, Ell started off on a different track.

Things are different now since I declared my Trace. I feel like less of a child. It's been weeks since I've daydreamt of Lord Blackworth and his shining soldiers. After that night, I stopped fantasizing about such things. They...they lost their luster.

I don't mean my Trace Declaration—I mean the night Gwen and I were attacked by the slaver. That was the night I realized that violence isn't something to lust after. I felt that man's hand on my arm while I was running away, and...I thought I was done. I thought I would die at age fourteen, alone.

I haven't told anyone that. Gwen would laugh at me, and so would Grandpa Em. I worry that Mum and Papa wouldn't understand—they didn't believe what we told them about the winking man. They thought he was just a regular old slaver, but...he couldn't be. Could he?

You must know, Grist. Why didn't the Kaene's fire seem to bother him? Why did he grab Gwen and not me?

Gwen. The word was like music or glass breaking. He couldn't tell which. *Things are different now, after the Declaration. We're acting differently, both of us. At first, I thought it was just the fact that we both had Traces to follow and were adjusting to that, but now...we've adjusted, and things are still...well, not bad. Just different.*

I never saw her as beautiful before, but now...it's all I see.

No, no, that's not it. That makes it sound like I don't still see her as brilliant and kind and funny and a good friend, it's just...I want to kiss her. I've never wanted that before.

What if she wants to kiss me? What if she doesn't *want to kiss me? I'd hoped it was just the adrenaline of the Declaration that made me think of her like that, but it's been two weeks. If anything, it's gotten worse. Every day, I see her, and I see my parents or another married couple and think 'could we...maybe?'* Multiple times before, he'd caught her staring up at him and blushing when their eyes met. She smiled when he told jokes, even ones that weren't funny. And she'd started saving him a seat next to her during breakfasts in the morning. *Does she like me as much as I like her?* The idea filled him with such elation, he resisted dwelling on it in fear of disappointing himself in the future.

It's terrifying, he prayed. *I don't know what to do. What can I do? I'm past the point of denial by now.*

I suppose...I suppose I just Persevere. Persevere through the anxiety and fear, and maybe one day, things will make sense again.

Five prayers—one hundred and fifty days—passed from the day of the Trace Declaration when it finally was brought into reality. Not in the way he'd expected, and not in the way he'd have preferred, but it happened.

They were on the road. Ellison and Gwenli were sitting together one night around the campfire. The other adults had all gone off to bed except for a handful, who were chatting sleepily about this and that just out of earshot.

The firelight cast shadows on Gwen's face like it had on the night of the Trace Announcement. It was like the darkness and light danced a duet across her skin, and Ellison found himself all too easily distracted by their dance.

"What do you think we'll do when we get older?"

"What?" Ell broke the daze. "I don't know...I suppose I'll take Papa's place. I'll run the caravan, if he'd like me to."

"Is that what you want to do?" she asked.

"I suppose," he answered. "I haven't much thought about what I want to do. Have you?" He knew the answer, but he also knew that she was dying for him to ask.

"Well," Gwenli began, "I don't know exactly what it is that I want to do, but I know I want to learn things. You know, Curiosity and all that. I guess it isn't just about Curiosity; I'm not building my future just off of my Trace, but it certainly helps to inform the decision.

"I'm not sure I want to stay with the caravan, but I don't want to be like Aunt Estaia," she continued. "My mama still barely speaks to her, even when we're in town. I'm worried she'll turn on me like that, and I don't want to bear that."

Aunt Estaia was Gwenli's aunt on her mother's side. Ellison had only met her once before when he was rather young. She'd grown up with the caravan and left to live on her own in the city of Enthcas. The caravan passed through Enthcas every year, but Estaia didn't make a point to check in. There were some poor relations there, and all Ellison knew was that it related to something Estaia had done before she'd left the caravan.

"I'm sure you won't end up like her," Ellison replied. "She's a bit...well, Grandpa Em says she did something to upset a few of the adults when she left. Just don't do anything like that."

Gwenli shrugged. "I guess that's true. But I don't really know what I want to do. Just that I want to learn and create. Maybe I'll write, maybe I'll learn to sculpt or paint. Maybe I could become a singer or play the lyre. And learn, I want to learn everything." She sighed. "I don't know. There's a lot of choices."

"There are. So…when do you think you'll leave the caravan?" He tried to keep the disappointment out of his voice.

"Relax," Gwenli laughed. "You aren't getting rid of me that soon. I guess I'll leave in a few years—but only when I feel ready. I always envisioned it being somewhere near my twentieth birthday, but—oh, I don't know. Maybe I won't leave at all."

Five years, he thought. *Five years is still a lot. Perhaps…*
Perhaps what? What are you wishing for, Ellison?

He didn't know the exact answer. Or maybe he did, and he didn't want to admit it. "Which city do you think it'll be? When you leave?"

"Aelos, I suppose," she answered with a speed that told him she'd been thinking about this for quite some time. "There's always Enthcas, too—maybe I could learn under Aunt Estaia for a while, then strike out on my own after a few years."

Ell nodded, attempting a look of nonchalance. "Sounds very…exciting. I'll miss you, Gwen."

She is never going to love you like you love her.

"I'll miss you too, Ellison," she murmured. His eyes were on the fire and he didn't see her face, but after a moment, he heard her inhale.

"What is it?" he asked, turning to her.

"What if you came with me?" she said.

He almost froze. "What if I did?"

"We could be friends."

"Friends," he repeated. *And there it is. She said it herself, that's all you'll ever be. Friends.*

"Or more," Gwen added hastily, seeing his face fall.
"More?"

"I—er—yes," she muttered, flushing. "Sorry, I didn't mean—I hope you weren't thinking…it's just that I—"

Look at her. Look how awkward she is. You're making her uncomfortable, Ellison.

56

"I—I'd better be getting to bed," she murmured, standing. "I..."

You're driving her away.

She started walking back to the wagons slowly. Ellison felt the same paralyzing fear in his heart that he'd felt on that night in Aelos, the night he'd almost lost Gwen.

No. Not again.

"Gwenli?"

She spun immediately. "What?"

Ellison crossed the distance between them without knowing it. The voice in his head tried to speak, but he ignored it.

Without another second's pause, he leaned forward and kissed her.

She didn't pull back. He stayed where he was, eyes half-closed, afraid to move and damage the situation. Gwen's hands were on his face, and his were on her waist, though he had no recollection of putting them there.

She pulled away and looked up at him. He stared quietly, the taste of her mouth fresh on his lips. "I love you," he murmured.

"I love you, too." They stayed like that, holding each other, until the fire burned down.

Chapter 10
Lief

"Do you think you'll marry her?" the little boy asked.

It had been three years since Ell and Gwen's Trace Declarations. The two of them were now eighteen years of age, well into adulthood by caravanners' standards. They'd been courting all the while, after that night by the fire.

That night at the fire had been the start of things. At first, their fledgling romance had been the talk of the troupe. It calmed down, though, as everyone realized Gwen and Ell's relationship wasn't some royal engagement to read about on the city newsboards. They were just…close. They were courting, and, perhaps, if it went well, they might ask one another to marry.

Ell had never felt more comfortable with anyone than he did with Gwen. He told her everything, and she did the same. They knew how the other thought, how they felt about everything. The intimacy was thrilling and simple, rare and ordinary all at once. And he would've had it no other way.

Today, Ellison walked beside his family's wagon, next to Mum and one of the littler children—Mars and Alisse's oldest, a boy named Lief. Little Lief, they called him. He had sandy blonde hair and freckles across his cheeks and a tendency to ask questions, much like Gwenli in her earlier years.

"I suppose so, Lief," Ell replied. "Not yet, though."

"Why not?" The boy was always ready with the next question. He could keep you going for hours if you had the patience. Ellison found it a good way to exercise Perseverance. Perhaps Lief could be annoying, but that was part of growing up.

"Because," he began, "We're waiting to make sure we're the right ones for each other."

Lief wrinkled his nose. "What does that mean?"

"It means," Mum explained, "well, some people get along very well. Like you and your sister." It was well-known that Lief and his twin sister, Andra, were close as petals on a rose. "But others don't. Ellison and Gwenli are simply making sure that they get along very well. They wouldn't want to marry and make a commitment, only to realize that they don't like each other as much as they thought."

"Oh," Lief shrugged. "Okay." After a moment, he said, "That's not why they get married in the stories."

"What?"

"In the stories, the kings marry the queens because the queens have a lot of money and their papas and mamas tell them to," Lief explained.

"Sometimes, yes," said Ellison. "Kings and queens, princes and princesses, they marry each other to bring their country more wealth. To make alliances—" Ellison saw the boy's eyebrows draw together and hastily simplified "—er, deals together with other countries. To make their people safer or happier. But those who aren't royalty don't have to worry about their country. They can marry whoever they want, like the Aesek says."

"So…that's why you are going to marry Gwenli?"

"That's why he's courting Gwenli," Mum corrected, with a wink in Ellison's direction.

You have to admit, Ellison thought, *he might be a little bothersome, but it can't be said that he's ever asked a question he didn't care to hear the answer to.*

"Where are we going?" Lief asked.

"Enthcas," Mum replied. "In fact, I think we're nearly there. Another hour or two." They'd been travelling for two weeks now, and all of them were itching to get off the road.

At this, Lief's eyes widened. "Almost there?! Really?"

"Do you remember Enthcas, little Lief?" Ellison asked. "We stopped there last year. That was when you and your mum both were sick with the burngasp malady."

He shook his head. "What's it like?"

"It's bordering the Northern Syentre Forest, so it's rather green," Mum told the child. "It's ruled by a Chieftain—Balovar Amicus is his name—and split into districts. Like Aelos, remember?"

"I remember. What are the districts' names?"

"You'll have to ask Ellison's father," she said. "He knows all those sorts of things."

"Hmm. Okay," Lief nodded. "What are we going to Enthcas for? Selling or buying?"

"It will be a sell-week when we arrive," Ell told Lief. "Then after this, we head north through the mountains to the next city. That's where we'll buy up our next round of goods."

"How long are we going to be staying in Enthcas?" Lief asked.

"Perhaps two weeks or so," Ell said. "Long enough for Pentelaud to pass over."

"What's Pentelaud?" The question was out before Ellison's sentence was done.

This would be a big one. In truth, Ellison and his mother had both avoided using the word around Lief, because they knew it would entail an immediate long and detailed explanation to the child. Ell hadn't even noticed he'd done it this time until it was out of his mouth.

Mum rolled her eyes at Ellison and began. "Well, Pentelaud is a single week on the Fayan Calendar—five days, remember?" Lief had just been taught how to count by the traditional Fayan Calendar system. "It's right at the end of every year, and it's a celebration. A celebration of Aesekra."

"Like a festival?"

"Yes," Ell picked up. "Very much like a festival. Cities all over Reqius throw Pentelaud festivities. You've seen them before; you just didn't know what they were for. It was last winter, when we were in Tespael and the troupe of musicians performed through the streets? There was candies and dances and all that. Do you remember?"

"Oh, yes!" Lief smiled. "What is it for?"

"Pentelaud is a special time that grown-ups take to pray to their Celestim every morning, instead of just once every thirty days like usual. There's great theatrical story-tellings every night, stories from the Aesek. They tell them on street corners, they act them out in city squares...it's a beautiful sight."

"When—how soon is it?" Lief asked. His eyes were glittering with excitement.

"We have five days until Pentelaud begins. We'll arrive at Enthcas by the end of today and sell for four days." All the families of the countryside, and those who lived on their own came into the city for the celebration. It was also a yearly time of trade and restocking for farmhouse supplies and the like. The caravan made very, very good money during Pentelaud because cities tended to be overcrowded with country people looking to buy the sort of things Ellison and his family were selling.

"Why is Pentelaud so important?" Lief asked.

"Like I said, it's a time for adults to pray to their Celestim more often, but it's also a time for teaching, for stories, for all sorts of things," Ell said.

"What kind of stories?"

Ellison smiled. "All sorts," he replied. "There's the tale of the Firion's Crippling—that's usually told on the very last night, and it's the grandest night of all. Last year, I heard the story of Magerson Who Broke His Trace, and—"

"Broke his Trace?" Lief interrupted. "How do you break a Trace? I thought they weren't real things."

"They aren't material," Mum corrected, "but that doesn't mean they aren't real. Breaking a Trace is an adult way of saying 'disobeying a Trace'."

"But…" Lief frowned, a finger to his lips, "My momma said people disobey their Traces all the time."

"Sure," Ell began, "people break their Traces often, but not like Magerson. He disobeyed his Trace intentionally—he *wanted* to. He didn't feel guilt or regret afterwards."

"Why not?"

"Well…" he paused. "It's a long story. I'm not sure I can explain a part of it without you knowing all of it."

"Can I ask Grandpa Em to tell it tonight?" Lief asked.

Ellison glanced sidelong at his mother. "I don't think so," he replied. "Grandpa Em hasn't been in the mood to tell many stories."

Grandma Elise had passed two prayers back. Nobody knew exactly what had killed her, but they'd decided to say it was the age. She'd always suffered a pain in her chest in the winter, and this time, it had just been too much. Grandpa Em had kept to himself ever since. Ellison and the others tried to talk to him, but Papa said he needed time.

"You know," Ell began, "if you'd like, I can try to tell the story myself."

Lief's face lit up. "You know it?"

"Well enough," he shrugged. "I've heard it a few times. And we've got some time left before we arrive in Enthcas. If anyone asks, tell 'em it was your lesson for the day."

"Yes, yes," Lief nodded. "Go ahead, I'll listen!"

Ell chuckled. "Alright, then. This, little Lief, is the tale of Magerson Who Broke His Trace."

Chapter 11
Magerson Who Broke His Trace

"Magerson was a good Aesekri man in his day—he Traced Humility, as some of our own do. He lived in Faya, in the days before Caraspen was formed, and lived in the city of Tespael with his wife and three children. His wife Traced Rationality, and his children Traced Patience, Loyalty, and Awe. It is *very* important that you remember that.

"Magerson and his family were happy. They worked hard, followed their Traces, and were prosperous.

"But tragedy struck. Magerson lived during the years of the Fayan War, and when it came time for battle, he was summoned to take up arms and join the fray. With honor and Humility, he bode his family farewell and joined the soldiers in fighting for Tespael's sovereignty.

"Magerson marched for years as a soldier. When the hostilities were ended and the war over, Magerson was overjoyed. He would at last be able to return home to his family! He went to his superior officer and asked if he was allowed to go home."

Ellison paused and looked at Lief, listening with rapt attention. "What do you think the officer said to Magerson?"

Lief was quiet. "Um...no?"

"That's right. This officer was a greedy man—he Traced Ambition, in fact. He was selfish and sneaky, and he knew that Magerson Traced Humility, so he was obligated to be humble to those above him. And the officer decided to take advantage of that.

"So, the officer lied to Magerson and said that he'd been given orders to make Magerson his own personal assistant, and that Magerson was to follow him back to his home to serve him there.

"At this, Magerson's heart cried out with longing for his family. However, he swallowed his anger and replaced it with Humility. 'I will serve you for as long as you wish,' he said. And he did. Magerson served the officer for seventeen years—long after the war's end, he was still separated from his family. Every day, he longed to return to his wife and his beloved children, but he was bound by his Trace to be humble.

"At the end of these seventeen years, Magerson's master died, and rule of the house passed to his son, a much kinder man. The son gave Magerson his freedom, and without a day's wait, Magerson set off for Tespael and his family.

"He travelled swiftly, sparing barely a second for sleep." Ell picked up his voice, talking faster. "When, at last, he came upon his beloved city, he found it just as he'd left it, and his heart sung. Rushing through the streets toward his home, he swung open the door and found a family he'd never seen before.

" 'Who are you, and where is my family?' he asked.

" 'This is our home!' the family replied. 'What are you doing here?'

"At this, Magerson grew angry. 'This is *my* home! Where are the people who lived here before you? A woman and three children—they were my family!'

" 'Oh,' the family said. 'They have long since passed. They starved to death in a long, frigid winter.'

"Magerson's heart broke. 'My family is dead?' He left the home, numb.

"Now, at this time, Magerson began to realize that all of the pain he'd felt over the past seventeen years, and the pain of losing his beloved family—it had all stemmed from his Trace. If he hadn't been so Humble, he wouldn't have served the officer for seventeen years, leaving his family to starve.

"Full of rage and frustration, Magerson sought revenge. 'But where from?' he thought. 'Not from the officer who enslaved me—he's already dead. Not from the family who took my home—it wasn't their fault that I wasn't there to help provide for my children.' Magerson was confused. 'If not from either of them, then from whom does this suffering stem?'

"Slowly, Magerson's eyes turned to the sky. 'You,' he hissed. 'Celestim—you have brought this on me! My Trace has brought me too much sorrow. You instructed me to be humble and follow that officer. If I had never kept my Trace, my family would still be alive!"

"Magerson began to think to himself. 'I must get revenge on them for the pain they have caused me. I will make them suffer.'

"The Celestim saw this act of evil and insubordination. They watched as Magerson spent the rest of his days breaking his Trace in any way possible—allowing *no* authority to tell him what to do. The mortal rulers of his nation attempted to capture and imprison him, but his rage was too strong. They could do nothing to stop this man who would submit to no one. The Celestim grew angry. When, finally, his acts of heresy grew too horrible to allow, Lady Rene, Celestim of Peace and Steward of Celestia, commanded the Celestim of Vigilance to strike Magerson down and bring him before the Celestim.

"At that moment, Magerson was scorched from Reqius and was brought before the Celestim. He stood before the twenty-three of them, arrayed in all of their splendor and glory.

" 'Magerson, breaker of your Trace,' Lady Rene began, 'you have brought great dishonor on yourself and your descendants. Why have you done this?'

" 'In rebellion against the Celestim,' Magerson said, 'for you taught me to follow my Trace, and it was because of that that my family died.'

" 'Mortal, have you considered that our motives are higher than pleasing you?' Rene asked.

"Magerson refused to give in. 'I asked never for myself to be pleased—only for my family to be happy.'

" 'And what if they *are*?' asked the Celestim of Rationality.

"Magerson faltered. He had not considered that. 'They are dead. How could they be happy?' But as soon as he said it, he paused. The voice of the Celestim of Rationality had sounded oddly familiar to him.

" 'You are…' he said. 'You are my wife!' "

Ellison glanced down at Lief. "Remember? I said it was important. His wife Traced Rationality. What did his children Trace?"

"Patience, Loyalty, and…oh, it was—"

"Awe," Mum supplied.

"That's right," Ell nodded. "Very good, little Lief. Now, back to our tale.

"The Celestim of Rationality nodded. 'In my mortal life, I *was* married to the mortal Magerson.'

" 'What of our children—where are they?' Magerson asked.

" 'We are here, he who was our father,' said the Celestim of Loyalty, Patience, and Awe.

" 'My children!' Magerson exclaimed. 'You are here! You have achieved the True Victory!'

" 'Yes, he who was our father. We followed our Traces even to death, and thus have been given the ultimate reward. You, however…you have not. You have committed the worst of sins.'

"Lady Rene continued. 'Magerson, you have broken your Trace, and for that, you must be punished. To the Void with you.'

"Magerson cried out for mercy, but he had done it all to himself. And so, Magerson who broke his Trace was sentenced to the Void, of which little is known.

"But let this be a warning, listeners. To break your Trace is to bring upon yourself certain death. Even Magerson, who thought he was justified, suffers in the Void for his sins."

Chapter 12
Enthcas

When they entered the city, Ellison walked next to Gwen. The experience of seeing a bustling city full of people all smiling and bustling about was one of her favorite things, and he liked to watch her marvel at the sights.

The caravan had a slow time of things once they got past Enthcas's gates. The entire city was crowded—it was Pentelaud, and as if that wasn't enough, the Monarchs were attending in Enthcas this year. Everyone and their best livestock wanted to sneak a glance at one of the Monarchs, which put the city at maximum capacity. The streets were crowded and it took them a good while to make it to the district they would be staying in.

As they walked, Ellison heard his name called down the line of wagons. "Send him up!" the voices echoed. "Tell Ellison his father's calling for him!"

He left Gwen's side and pushed to the front. His father walked with a hand on the horse's reins, guiding them through the bustling street. As Ellison came up beside him, Papa said, "Go ahead and make sure our tavern is ready for us. We can't take up all the street space for too long once we get there or there'll be fines to pay."

Ellison nodded. "What's it called?"

"*The Arborman's Haven*," Papa replied. "About ten minutes up this street. Big red sign above the door, you'll know it. Owner's name is Gon. Take Gwen."

"That's not the deal we agreed upon," the tavernkeeper grumbled from behind the bar.

"The deal we agreed upon is two years old, Gon," Ell replied, his arms folded. "And even if we had agreed to a set price, which we *didn't*, there'd be no way of holding to it. Rates change, you know as well as I do."

"We've got thirty-odd coming your way," Gwen added. "They'll be here in three minutes. If we don't have a deal by then, they'll just keep moving down the street to the next tavern. There's plenty of other places in the Enthcas who'd love the business."

"Then why don't you take it there?" Gon snapped.

"We might," Gwen shrugged. "But we've done business with you for the past few years, and you've been good to us. Good hospitality."

"Which is why my prices lie where they do," the man snapped.

He's not bad at this, Ellison thought. "Gon, our numbers have gone up—Two new little ones, and a new family joined up two prayers back. What you lose in room pay you'll make up for tenfold in food and drink alone. Not to mention, we're hoping to make a large profit since it's Pentelaud. We'll be able to tip quite heavily before we leave."

The man's eyebrows arched before he caught himself. He stared at them, chewing his lip and rocking on his heels.

"We don't have all day," Gwen pushed.

"Fine, fine," he sighed, leaning forward against the bar. "You promise a nice fat gift, a thank you, maybe—then perhaps we can talk."

Ell smiled. "That's it. Thank you, Gon. I knew you'd come around. In fact, you know what? We've got a boy, Marin, he's not too bad with a lute. I'll talk to him, see if he can't maybe play a few songs 'round dinner time each night."

"Everyone knows a tavern with music's sweeter than one without," Gwen added. "So, what'll be the price?"

After the payment was settled, Ell and Gwen went back up the street with Gon to the stables where they could block the wagons for the night. They easily guided the caravan in and Ell let his father know the price they'd settled on.

Papa let out a low whistle. "You and Gwen are getting good at this. I remember back when your mother and I were like that. She was so sly...she'd bat those big brown eyes and the men would fall over. Worked like a charm."

Ell laughed. "How long ago was that?"

"Oh, long before you were born," Papa chuckled. "Good work, my boy. You and she will make good caravan leaders one day."

Ell had never mentioned to his father Gwen's desire to eventually leave the caravan—nor the fact that if she did, Ellison would follow her. He knew it would break the old man's heart to know that his son might not take the family duties as he'd been raised to, and anyways, Gwen might still decide to stay.

That night, once the rest of the caravan had turned in, Ellison slipped out of his parents' and his room, sneaking into the taproom.

It was dark—Gon had gone to bed as well, and the front door was locked. The pure quiet was unnerving.

It was rare that Ellison found himself fully alone, in an environment of complete silence. There were no frogs croaking, birds calling, no wagon wheels crunching through gravel and dirt. The fire had been put out, and in its place was raw, unadulterated silence.

"Good work today," Gwen said.

"Drast!" he jumped. "You scared me, girl."

She had been hiding by a table in the corner "That was my plan," she laughed, crossing the room to him. "Good evening."

"Good evening," he smiled, stepping closer to her and wrapping his arms around her waist.

She beamed and brought her lips up to meet his. She tasted of spice, a remnant of the dinner they'd shared. "I love you," she whispered.

He brought a hand up to her hair and fumbled at the tie of her braid. "I love you too, dear." Her hair fell down her back, golden blonde curls tumbling across her shoulders.

She kissed him again, deeply, then broke off. He felt her stiffen in his arms and released her immediately. "What is it?"

"I..." she put her forehead to his chest. "I was thinking about something earlier on the road."

"Are you alright, darling?" He sat down in one of the booths, Gwen sliding in next to him.

"Yes, I'm fine," she nodded. And then, all of a sudden, "Remember when we met the Monarchs? That horrible night?"

Ellison shivered. The figure in black had never left his imagination. The wink, the cackle, the fire. Every few prayers, Gwen had nightmares that woke Ellison up.

"Do you remember what the woman—the Kaene—what she did to him?" said Gwen. "He caught on fire and laughed."

"Yeah," Ell murmured. He didn't like to admit how often he still thought about it all.

"I want to find him," Gwen said, leaning her head against his shoulder.

"What?"

"I want to find him and make him pay. It can't be impossible, right? We were lucky to escape, but what if we hadn't? I can't live knowing there are other people out there who might suffer because of this man," she muttered.

Ellison was quiet for a while. "It could be dangerous."

"I know."

"Wouldn't it be better to just forget? It's over now, dear."

She sighed. "It's over, but it's not finished. And you're confusing better with safer."

He smiled. "Then yes, I suppose you're right. Do it, brilliant girl. But I'm staying by your side the entire way."

"Good," she smiled. "Oh, I was so worried about what you'd say. I just...I can't keep living with the knowledge that he's out there, probably hurting other people."

"What do you plan to do with him," Ellison asked. "Once you've found him, of course."

"I'll inform the Law-Watchers, the police forces, anyone who will listen," she explained. "Then it's over, I promise."

He nodded. "Okay. Do you have a plan for tracking him down?"

"Yes," she smiled. "And it starts in Enthcas." She stood and crossed her arms. "There's someone here I want to ask some questions of. Someone who knows more than either of us about the Monarchs, magics, and probably that man."

"And who is that?"

Chapter 13
Pentelaud

The caravan spent three long days selling everything they'd purchased and made in the prayers past. From sun-up to sundown, their wagons were open for trade.

Papa had explained to Ellison that Enthcas would likely be their most profitable stop of the entire year due to Pentelaud, but not even he had predicted the margin of wealth they accumulated by the end of the sell-week. They had expected to stay open for the four days leading up to Pentelaud, but by the end of the third, almost all the caravans were sold out. It had been years since Ellison saw one of the wagons run out of wares, but by the end of the third day, all but five had closed down.

After the third night, as the caravanners all sat in the taproom of *The Arborman's Haven*, Papa called their attention to a change in the plans. Tomorrow, all sell-able items would be moved to his and Mum's wagon, and they would continue selling. Everyone else could have the day free. *Explore Enthcas,* he said. *We've had a hard year of work. You all deserve a few days to relax.*

Ellison locked eyes with Gwen—they were thinking the same thing. As Papa sat back down, he crossed the room to her.

They sat in the corner by the stairwell. He lowered his voice and spoke. "If we're going to see Aunt Estaia, we should do it tomorrow, don't you think?" True, he felt slightly guilty leaving his parents to work all day while he and the rest of the caravan relaxed, but Gwen deserved her answers.

"I suppose…I was planning on doing it during the first night, during the Pentelaud festivities," said Gwen.

"Not tomorrow, then?" Ellison frowned. "I thought you really wanted to know, Gwen. We might not get a chance as good as this again."

"I know…" she sighed, absently fingering her braid. "You—I don't know."

"It's okay, love. We can wait."

"No, no, it's not—it's not that. I promise," she said. "I just feel a little guilty. I'd feel bad doing all that while your parents work. They deserve the rest more than us, right? I don't know, I just…"

Ellison sat back and ran a hand through his hair. "I love you."

"What?"

"I love you," he smiled. "Firion, but I was thinking the exact same thing, I just figured you'd want to use the day to meet Aunt Estaia."

"I did at first, but I feel a little guilty. I don't want to leave your parents to work while we wander off."

Ellison leaned over and kissed her on the cheek. "Is it okay if I ask my father to take the duties myself?" Ellison asked.

"Only if I can join you," she winked.

It took some convincing, but by the time they turned in, Ellison had wrestled the responsibility of operating the sell-wagon from his father. He and Gwen would take up the duties themselves, and Mum and Papa would have the day free.

And so on the fourth day in Enthcas, Ellison and Gwenli woke early to take the last wagon to market. Gwen suggested a competition, so they played a game—in the morning, they split all the goods and competed for profits.

By noon, though, they were both bored of their solo endeavors and made a new plan. After a quick mid-day meal, they put their goods together and sold as a team. After that, it only took a few hours for the wagon to empty. They packed up and returned it to its place near the stables before dusk.

Ellison and Gwenli had discussed the specifics of their plan for finding and meeting Estaia earlier. That night, they went to the edge of the district gate, where the great newsboards and bulletins and city censuses were stationed. After that, it was only a few minutes before they located the address of *Lovedale Apothecary*, which Gwen was convinced belonged to her rogue aunt.

The festivities of Pentelaud would begin at midnight. If Ell and Gwen were going to sneak away and meet Gwen's aunt, that would be the best time to do it—in the darkness, while the rest of the city was preoccupied with the ceremonies and revelry.

They returned to their rooms to wait.

Ellison was woken by a massive boom and a flash of light.

"It's starting!" Mum was already awake, looking out the window.

All of a sudden, Ellison heard a sound like rushing waves or thunder. The city was cheering. The entire city. Thousands of people, he imagined. All for one moment, all unified in a single act. Raising their voices.

Ell's father drew near to the window and looked down into the city. "Happy Pentelaud, dear," he smiled. "Let's go down into the street. Come on, both of you!"

They could already hear the rest of the caravanners in the hallway—little Lief's voice squealing with glee, and his mother's stern warnings for him to slow down.

"I'm going to go find Gwen," Ellison said to his parents. "I'll meet you in the street."

"Don't be long," his mother said as she and Papa slipped out the door.

Ellison waited until the hallway was quiet again, then stepped out of the room.

Just as they'd planned, Gwen was waiting in the taproom. She wore her cloak and carried a lantern they'd grabbed off of one of the wagons a few hours ago. "Ready?"

"Ready," he nodded. "Let's go."

Ellison had never seen anything like this before. The street outside was crowded with people. He and Gwenli almost had trouble getting out the tavern's front door. When they were outside, Gwen slipped her hand into Ell's and they pushed against the movement of the crowd. She had memorized the route to Estaia's earlier, while he slept.

A dozen different melodies, played by three dozen different instruments and carried on a hundred separate voices, filled the air. On every block, a performer or musician was leading the people in a different Pentelaud hymn. The Enthcans sang with a joviality that made Ellison want to stop and join in.

It took about ten minutes of pushing against the crowd for Ellison and Gwen to break free. They turned a corner onto a darker street, not wide enough to warrant being lit by oil-lamps. It was almost black, but Gwen had planned ahead. She reached into her jacket and pulled out a small lantern, along with the matchbox she'd purchased earlier in the day. After a second, the space around them was illuminated with warm golden light. "This way," Gwen whispered, setting off again.

The farther they went, the quieter the mirth rang. Ellison felt a shiver as it faded fully, leaving them in silence. They were far from their tavern now.

"We're getting close," Gwen whispered, the excitement in her tone almost palpable.

How is she not afraid?

Ellison tensed as they walked. Gwen's swaying lamp illuminated the forms of sleeping beggars and addicts curled in corners or alleys. He flashed back to the memory of the man who winked, back in Aelos, and suddenly had an overwhelming desire to check behind them for assailants, but he knew that if he did it once, he wouldn't be able to stop. *Persevere,* he told himself. *Relax. Persevere. Don't be irrational.*

Gwen's voice pulled him out of his trance. "Ell?"

He bumped into her, only now noticing that she'd stopped walking and was standing in the street before a shop. "I think we're here."

Indeed, a sign hung by the door that read *Lovedale Apothecary.* Ellison felt his heartbeat pick up. "Remember the last time you convinced me to sneak out into a city without telling our parents?"

"Yeah," Gwen murmured. "Why do you mention it?"

He rocked on his heels. "Er, no reason."

"Honestly, love, you worry too much. What could go wrong?" She winked and knocked hard on the door.

Chapter 14
Aunt Estaia's House

There was no response.

Ellison glanced nervously down the street, but the night was silent. From deeper into the city, he saw a brief flash of light—a firework, probably, or a trick of the theatre. *So far away,* he thought.

"I want to ask you a few questions," Gwen called, knocking again. "Please, can you open the door? I'm Gwenli Asfina, your niece? Please, I just have a few questions."

Again, silence.

"Alright," she sighed. "Nobody home. I suppose she's—"

The door cracked open and Gwenli froze mid-sentence. "Quiet," a voice hissed from within. "Who's the boy?"

Gwen's hand unconsciously sook for Ellison's. "My…my parnter," she squeaked. "My friend. Ellison Blackworth. He's Hanik and Issela's—"

"I know Ellison," the voice snapped. "I was there for his birth. I helped deliver him."

Ellison shivered. "Can we…can we come in?"

Silence.

"Please?" Gwen asked. "We have questions about…well, about a lot."

"Fine." The door swung open and revealed a petite woman. She had blonde hair like Gwen, cut to her shoulders in the style that indicated betrothal, but not yet marriage. Her figure was slim, and she wore a thin gossamer dress, a heavy blanket draped over her shoulders. A pair of spectacles rested on her temple, and she stood with arms folded, examining the two young people. "My name is Estaia Lovedale. Follow me."

She turned and gestured them in towards a set of stairs going up. They followed her silently. Ellison's heart thundered. Ahead, Gwen looked remarkably calm.

Estaia didn't break the silence as they walked, and Ell found himself panicking. "So," he began, "You're betrothed? That's, er, that's lovely. How long until you're married?"

"What?" she frowned. "Oh my breathing days, no. I'm not betrothed. I just got sick of hair in my face and figured I shouldn't let some centuries-old habit dictate how I carry myself every day."

Ell blinked. "Oh. I…sorry. I didn't mean to offend you."

"Firion Crippled and every Celestim in the sky," she swore, "isn't he his father's son…"

"What do you mean?"

"Aunt Estaia, thank you for letting us come in," Gwen interrupted as they entered a large room. There were bookshelves against one end and a large circular table with the center cut out in the middle of the room. Estaia walked over to an end table with a glass of what Ellison assumed to be alcohol on it and took a sip.

"Your questions, child?" She gestured expectantly, a hand on her hip. "Let's hear them."

"Oh, um—right. Well, that's…," Gwen murmured, fiddling with her braid. "I suppose—"

"Why did you leave the caravan?" Ellison asked.

"Oh, and there's your mother in you," Estaia snorted.

Ellison ignored her. "Can you answer the question or not?"

She gave him a long, measured look and said, "I left because I didn't feel like staying."

"That's not an answer."

"Oh, wonderful," she said with a dry glare. "I left because I didn't want to spend my life wandering, always being good at some things but never the best at anything. I wanted to be a scientist, a researcher, an inventor. So I did it."

"That's it? You wanted to work?" he asked.

"That's why I brought up leaving, yes," Estaia said, shifting.

"That doesn't seem like enough reason for our parents to not want to talk to you anymore," Ellison frowned.

Gwen shot him a warning glance, but he couldn't tell for what. "Aunt Estaia, we—"

Estaia silenced Gwen with a wave. "Let me say this, boy. If you want to know why your parents hate me, the answer is in easy sight. I've already given it to you, in fact."

"What do you mean?" he frowned. Gwen looked uneasy again.

She sighed. "Why am I here and not down there with the rest of the peasantry, dancing and screaming at the sky?"

Ellison was sure his cheeks were red with embarrassment. "I…I'm sorry, I don't know."

She looked to Gwen. "Go ahead, dear. Tell him. It's clear he's not going to figure it out on his own."

Gwen looked from Ellison to Estaia. "I—I don't think it's my place."

"Nonsense," Estaia snapped. "If you want my help with…whatever it is you need, you'll tell the boy."

Gwenli slowly turned to Ellison. "Love, Aunt Estaia is not celebrating Pentelaud because she…well, she doesn't—she's not Aesekri."

"What do you mean?"

"Oh, for Firion's sake!" Estaia burst. "He's slower than his father, and that man couldn't add two-digit numbers without his wife's help."

"That's enough," Ellison snapped. "I don't care how brilliant you think you are, don't insult my father."

Estaia paused. "Very well, boy." She took another sip of her drink. "Gwenli is right. I denounced Aesekra a year after both of you were born. I tried to be civil about it, but…they wouldn't listen."

Ellison felt his stomach tense. *Why would she…what? Who is this woman, and why would she do something so ridiculous as denounce Aesekra?*

"I tried to be reasonable," she continued. "I told them all that I didn't want to be pinned down to one thing. I had declared a Trace as a girl, but I found no fulfillment in it. Eventually, I had to threaten to Trace Lust or Recklessness for your parents to give up on me."

"But those—aren't those Nirrinic paths?"

Estaia nodded. "It was an empty threat, but I don't think they understood."

Ellison remembered the terse conversation he and Gwen had had years ago, on the ride into Aelos with Papa. Now, he understood why Papa had reacted so sharply when Gwen asked if he knew anyone who'd Traced Nirrinic paths. He'd been thinking of Estaia.

"How'd you figure it out?" Estaia asked Gwenli. "Did your mother tell you?"

Gwen shook her head. "I figured it out myself."

"How long ago?"

"About five minutes back, when you answered the door," she replied. "You've lived in Enthcas for years, there's no way you'd be home on the first night of Pentelaud—especially not this year, with the Monarchs and…"

Estaia gave her a proud look. "I'm impressed, though I should've expected it—you have my blood in you, girl. May I ask—it doesn't make much sense to come to my house at a time when you expected me to be gone, out in the streets. Why, then, did you try?"

Ellison hadn't even considered of such a thing, but now that Estaia mentioned it, it made perfect sense. Gwen looked at her feet. "I…I—I was planning on breaking in."

Estaia laughed. Ellison frowned. "Er—what? When were you going to tell *me* that?"

She gave him an apologetic look. "I'm sorry, Ell—I knew you wouldn't agree to come if I told you I was going to…."

"You wouldn't have made it through the door," said Estaia. "It's solid oak on four iron hinges and two padlocks. Then there's the staircase tripwires, the second-floor alarm…. Well, anyways, let's get to it. I don't have all night; what did you want to know?"

"Right," Gwen sighed. And so, she told Aunt Estaia the entirety of the tale of the man in black and their encounter with the Monarchs.

When the story was done, Estaia leaned back, took a sip of her whiskey and said, "That's a good one, my girl. How much of it is true?"

"All—all of it."

Estaia laughed. "Don't waste my time, love."

Gwenli grit her teeth. "I'm not. Can you help me or not?"

"You still have asked me no questions," Estaia noted.

84

"Who was the man?" Ellison asked. "Why did he not burn? How did the Monarchs set fire to him or heal Gwen? Where did they learn to do it? Could you help us find him?"

"There we are," she smiled. "I can't answer those all. I don't know who the man was. As to why he didn't burn, I'd wager he was wearing some sort of flame-resistant garment. They're not hard to find if you know where to look. I'd warrant he was a slaver of some sort, but it seems you've already gathered that much. Next question...oh, right. That's the easiest one. Isradellar Yesdas is a Caustisantic, loves." Ell remembered Isra using that term, but it still didn't mean much of anything to him.

"When Monarchs take office, they are gifted Cognisantic powers—Caustisia, Hemosia, Histosia, or Astrosia. This is because of a complicated and dense Enchantment cast by Quen Fairlon at Caraspen's founding, but that's not important. When Kaene Yesdas took office, she was given the powers of a Caustisantic. That's how she set fire to the man. It's simple, really. If one of you became a Monarch, there'd be a one-in-four chance you could do the same thing."

Ellison walked to the window as another firework went off in the distance. Behind him, Estaia continued. "As to how you might find him, I don't have a strong answer. But I have theories."

"Go ahead—please," Gwen said.

In the street below, Ellison could see a lantern light bobbing in one direction, held by a thin man wearing pressed clothes. He had a well-trimmed beard—married—and didn't seem to be in any sort of rush to get where he was going. As the girls talked behind him, Ellison watched the man moving on his way.

"Most slavers sell to two sorts of organizations," Estaia explained. "Military legions, for one—the Vahzese military is about one third enslaved men. But

85

when it's not to warlords and generals, slavers usually do business with rich families that live out in the countryside. Those they sell end up working as farmhands or kitchen maids…or worse."

"How does that help us to track him down?" Gwen asked.

"I'm afraid it's the most help I can give you," Estaia sighed. "I don't particularly recommend going about, asking if anyone's seen this man. He sounds more dangerous than I either of you could handle—no offense, of course."

Suddenly, the man below froze. Ellison frowned, leaning forward against the window to get a better look.

The well-dressed man was peering into the darkness at something down in the street. He spun, the lantern swaying and casting wild shadows on the shops and houses. *What's he seeing?*

"You could return to Aelos and see if you can lure him out," Estaia suggested. "Well, unless…"

"Unless what?"

She paused. "You're sure this is the only time either of you has seen this man?"

Below, the man whirled again. *Is he okay? What's he looking at?*

"I…I suppose so," Gwen murmured. "I think I'd remember something like that, otherwise."

A figure darted into the man's lantern light. He moved so fast, Ellison could barely get a good look at him. Before the well-dressed man could even flinch, the figure was atop him, the lantern cast aside and the street was plunged into darkness.

The next thought came without hesitation. *I have to help him.*

He took off out the door and down the staircase into the street.

"Ellison! Where—Ellison!" Gwen's voice called from back upstairs, but he was already out the door. He threw the bolt open and flung himself out into the street.

"Help!" a voice cried.

"Shut your mouth, old man!"

"Help! Someone, he—" the voice broke off in a whimper, immediately followed by a wet, blunt sound.

Ellison ran towards the cries. In the dim light, he had a split second to make out the figure of a man atop another man, beating him with a rock.

Without another breath, Ell sprung forward and grabbed the attacker around his waist, flinging him to the cobblestones. "Run!" he shouted to the victim. "Go!"

In the next instant, something solid slammed into his shoulder. Ellison screamed out in pain, thrashing blindly.

"I'll kill you too," the attacker growled. His breath was sharp and ragged.

Ellison threw his fist out, but the darkness blinded him and he punched through empty space. In that instant, the man connected the stone with Ellison's jaw, and he felt something crack.

Instead of pain, anger sparked within him. *Persevere.* The man had him pinned down. *Persevere.* With a surge of adrenaline, Ellison wrenched himself free. His shoulder burned and his jaw was afire, but he put his fists up. *Persevere.*

The man charged. At the last second, Ell threw himself to the side. The attacker stumbled, swinging through empty air, and Ell flung himself into the man's chest. The man slammed to the cobblestones and Ellison heard his head make a cracking sound on the pavement.

He fell onto the man, pinning him, and felt for the rock in his hand. When he had it, he ripped it from the man's hand and flung it aside. In a blind rage, Ellison drove his fist into the man's face once and again and again and again and again. His knuckles burned but he couldn't stop. *Persevere.*

He didn't know how long it took, but eventually Ellison realized that the man was still. He finally took a breath, chest heaving, his entire body aching. His jaw was split, his lungs burning. *I need to find Gwen.*

All of a sudden, something hit him from behind.

Ellison blacked out.

Chapter 15
Light

Ellison's first awareness was of cool air on his face.

He blinked his eyes open and squinted against sunlight—sunlight? That couldn't be right. It had been the dead of night before, when….

In a rush, everything came back to him—Gwen, Estaia, the mugging, the fight, and then…he looked around. *Where am I?*

He was alone in the room. It wasn't very large—just enough space for his bed and a table. There were three open glass windows on the wall opposite him, natural light pouring in.

The sheets of his bed were pure white and smelled of cleaning chemicals. *I'm in a hospital bed,* Ellison realized. *But I don't feel…hurt.* He looked himself over— the clothes he'd been wearing earlier were gone, replaced by a simple white gown.

I fought that man. There was blood. He cracked my jaw, didn't he? Ellison prodded at his jawbone and felt only a distant soreness.

The door swung open and in walked a woman in a pressed white dress. "Good morning, koso." She smelled of chemicals and sterilized utensils, the same as his bed. "How are you feeling?"

"I...where am I?" His mind felt like it was moving through sludge.

The woman smiled. She wore her hair down—married. "I am your nurse," she said. "You are in the infirmary of Keep Asselo. Your family is on their way. I don't think they'll be long."

"Keep Asselo..." The term sounded familiar. "Are we still in Enthcas?"

"Yes, koso." She seemed almost amused.

"What is it?"

"Keep Asselo is the living space of the Chieftain of Enthcas."

"Wait..." he frowned. "Why am I here? Did I do something wrong?"

"On the contrary, koso. You saved a life. An important one, in fact."

Before the nurse could continue, in stepped two figures. One was a rotund, red-cheeked man with glittering rings on every finger. The other was...

Isradellar Yesdas. The Kaene of Caraspen. "Good morning, Ellison. It's been a while."

Ellison felt his mouth dry up. "I—etsa Yesdas, I—I don't understand. Please, what did I do?"

Isra sat down on the edge of the bed. There was a familiar, gentle sympathy in her eyes. "Well, in simplest terms, you saved the life of the Surveyor's Secretary."

"Who?"

"The Surveyor of Caraspen, Arzen Graydrift."

That's another Monarch, Ellison realized. He'd heard the name before.

"The man you saved was the chief Secretary to the Surveyor," Isra explained. "All of our Secretaries travelled with us to Enthcas to celebrate Pentelaud. Simuin—that is the Secretary's name—was out on a night walk when he was attacked. You saved his life, Ellison."

"I…" Ellison's head spun. "I didn't mean to…to hurt anyone. Did I—"

Isra smiled again. "You aren't in trouble, Ellison. Simuin ran back to the Keep and told us what happened, so Balovar here," she gestured to the large man standing in silence, "sent some soldiers to see if they could help you. They ran into etsa Asfina—yes, Gwenli is okay—and she said that you needed help. We've been treating your wounds for the past day and half."

"My jaw," he said. "I think he broke my jaw. Why…"

"Why are you not in terrible pain?" she finished. "Do you remember Aelos, when first we met? Do you remember how Anroth's Hemosantic powers were able to heal etsa Asfina then? He used his magic to heal your jaw, your shoulder, and your fists. He was able to spare a lot of your pain." Beside her, the large man—Balovar—opened his mouth, but a rapid glare from Isra shut it again, and he just grumbled something under his breath.

Ellison sat back. "Okay. I…I don't know what to say. Thank you."

"Thank you, Ellison," said Isra. "I remembered you for so long after that night in Aelos. Both you and Gwen, in fact. You both stood out to me. And if I was impressed with you *then*," she laughed, "I consider it a privilege to have met someone like you twice in my lifetime, young man."

Ell flushed. "I—er—thank you, etsa."

All of a sudden, the door swung open again. Gwen burst in. Her cheeks were flushed, her hair askew. "He's awake?" Her eyes found Ellison, and she pushed past Isra to his side. "Oh, Ell! You're okay! I was so scared; what happened? You were there and then gone, I— what happened?" She cupped his face in her hands and kissed his forehead.

He smiled. "I'm alright, love. I'm okay."

91

"What happened?" Gwen repeated.

"Ellison saved a life," Isra answered. "He is a hero, Gwen."

Gwen beamed. "I know," she said, looking back at him. "I know he is." She kissed his cheek and took his hand, sitting on the edge of the bed.

"How are you feeling, son?" It was Papa's voice. Both his mother and father stood in the doorway next to the quiet fat man—the Chieftain, Balovar.

"I'm alright, Papa," Ell smiled. "I'm sorry if I scared you, we should've told you where we were going, I—"

"Don't apologize, love," his mother interrupted, joining Gwen at his bedside. "From what Gwen and the Kaene say, you did a good thing."

"I suppose," he nodded.

"He's far too humble," Isra laughed. "Your son is a hero. You both should be proud. You raised him well."

"Yes," Papa nodded, "Thank you, etsa."

Isra smiled and stood. "I'll leave you all now. The festivities are ongoing, and I am needed in less than an hour with the other three Monarchs." She turned to Ellison. "Thank you, young man. I believe the last we spoke, you were not old enough to declare a Trace. May I ask what you decided upon?"

"Perseverance," he answered.

She paused, then smiled. "A good choice, I think. Well then, Ellison…Persevere." With one final bow of her head, she slipped out the door. The Chieftain wasted no time in following her out.

A few hours later, Ellison was deemed healthy enough to leave the infirmary. The nurse explained that his clothes had been bloodied and were simply not wearable anymore, and that Isra had made arrangements for him to be fitted with a replacement outfit. Ell, Gwen, and his parents were led to another room where a tailor was waiting. The clothes were measured to his form and sewn on him. After an hour or two, the tailor was finished, and they were led to the Keep gates.

Anroth's magical healing had worked wonders. Ellison's pain was minimal—his jaw still ached, but his knuckles were healed over and the place where his forehead had bled was sealed.

They returned to the tavern and the rest of the caravan with a very good story to tell.

The rest of the day passed in a fever blur. Ell spent all of it with Gwen, enjoying the festivities. They didn't bring up Estaia until they were alone in their room the first night.

"Did you get any answers?" he asked.

"We stopped talking after you ran out," she explained. "She had a few ideas, but I wasn't certain about any of them. Though…there was one thing she said that's stuck with me."

"Oh? What's that?"

"She asked if Aelos was the only time we'd ever seen the man. And…I said no, but now I'm not sure," Gwen frowned.

Ell patted the bed, and she came and sat on the edge. Gently, he nudged her backward, and she laid her head on his lap. As he began to run his fingers through her hair, he said, "When do you think we could've met him before?"

"I don't *know*," she sighed, "and that's the scariest part. We didn't get a very good look at his face—he could be anyone, couldn't he? Anyone at all…."

"Wait a second," Ell paused. "What if—no, no."

"What?"

"I didn't remember until just now, but I won that fight. I did. I had the man pinned," he explained. "I watched him stop moving."

Gwen raised an eyebrow. "Are you bragging, Ellison Blackworth?"

"No—it just doesn't make sense. I blacked out."

"So?"

"Well, if the mugger was already out, and there was nobody else there, then who knocked me out?"

They locked eyes and waited for the other to say what they were both thinking. *Could it be him? The laughing man from Aelos?*

But it was too far-fetched, too unrealistic, too conspiratorial. "We'd sound like lunatics," Gwen sighed.

The conversation lapsed to silence.

They spent hours toying with different theories, each worse than the last.

"I'd hoped Estaia would have some more concrete advice on how to track him down," Gwen muttered.

"Estaia..." he said. "She was entertaining."

Gwen laughed. "I guess you could say that. Personally, I'd choose 'arrogant' or 'cruel', but *entertaining* works."

He laughed back, his fingers combing through her blonde hair. "I—nevermind."

"What?"

"Nothing," he said.

"*What?*" she insisted, sitting up.

"I was going to say she reminded me of you."

Gwen's face contorted in shock. "I hate you..."

"You love me," Ell sighed, kissing her on the cheek.

"Mmm...maybe I do." She turned and kissed him on the lips before pulling back to stare him in the eyes.

"Will you marry me?" The words were out of his mouth before he could catch them.

Gwen's eyes widened. "What?"

"I...will you marry me, Gwenli?"

Her eyes were locked with his. "Of course, I will."

94

He beamed. "Good." Ell leaned forward, pushed her back on the bed, and kissed her again. "I love you. I don't care if you leave the caravan or stay with it forever. I'll follow you wherever you go."

She smiled. "I'm never leaving you. I promise."

Chapter 16
Ceremony

Ell and Gwenli announced their betrothal on the last night of Pentelaud. After the festivities of the night—the caravan watched a musical retelling of Firion's Crippling and the banishing of the Nirrin—they returned to *The Arborman's Haven* as one great family.

When they woke the next morning, the rest of the city was still asleep. Merchants and grocers were already setting up shop in the squares, but most of Enthcas was recuperating after a week of incessant celebration. The caravanners were quite exhausted themselves, but they had work to do. They unblocked the wagons and set off out of the city with the practiced efficiency Ellison had grown so accustomed to.

Most of the children spent the day sleeping in the backs of the wagons. Ell and Gwen walked hand in hand, chatting and teasing each other. Tonight was their betrothal ceremony, during which Ellison's mother would cut Gwenli's braid, signifying the commitment Gwen had made to her son. When Gwen's hair grew down past her shoulders, it would be time for the wedding.

When the sun kissed the horizon and the caravan came to a flat clearing, Papa gave the call to block the wagons and prepare for camp. They worked like a seasoned ship-crew, everyone performing their tasks and working together to make sure that the job was complete as soon as possible. Within an hour, they sat around a blazing fire, sharing dinner—a stew with rabbit, carrot, potato, and barley.

Ellison sat between Grandpa Em and Gwenli. They chatted, teased, and laughed for a few minutes, but the air was anxious. Everyone in the caravan knew that the moment of Gwen's ceremony was fast approaching, and it wasn't long before Gwen's father cleared his throat and signaled for quiet.

"My friends, my family," he beamed, "we are gathered tonight to celebrate the union of two beloved members of our family—a man and woman that many of us have watched from their childhood. My daughter, Gwenli Asfina, and our resident hero, Ellison Blackworth." There was a round of cheers as he paused.

Ellison had taken on a sort of fame in the caravan after he returned from Keep Asselo, especially with the children. They thought of him as a legend—he'd met the Kaene! They were infatuated, too, with the soft material of his new tailored clothes. Lief kept saying it was soft as a chicken.

"Gwenli is my eldest daughter," her father continued, "and the first to commit to a betrothal. This is a very special night for me, and admittedly, a bittersweet one. I remember, as I'm sure many of you do, when little Gwen was just a toddler. I swear, her mother and I were so scared we were going to lose her—we went into Aelos when she was just three and I tied a rope from my wrist to hers to keep her from wandering." The caravan laughed, and Ellison saw Gwenli blush. "And do you know what she did?"

"She figured out how to untie the rope!" Grandpa Em called from beside Ellison.

A chorus of raucous laughter went up, and Ell nudged Gwen. She was shifting in her seat, and he put his hand on hers to calm her.

Her father continued. "At only three years old, she learned how to undo the knot so she could get away. Ellison, I hope you've got a better plan than I did for keeping her!"

Ell laughed. "I've given up trying to keep her down," he called. "Better to just let her go, like a cat. She usually comes back by dawn." The caravan exploded into laughter. Beside him, Gwen rolled her eyes.

When the cackles died down, Gwen's father spoke up again. "Now, on to more serious things. It makes me sad to watch my little girl grow up. I'd keep her with me forever and on if I could, but there's nobody I'd rather send her into the world with than Ellison. Son," he gestured, "you have my complete and honest blessing. She is yours."

"She is her own," Ellison smiled, "but thank you. I accept your blessing."

Her father nodded. "Now, it is time for the ceremony. Issela, please do the honor."

Ellison's mother stepped forward and held up a pair of scissors. "Come forward, Gwen."

Gwen glanced back at him, and he winked. She stood and walked over to Mum, who was waiting with the scissors.

There was a sound like branches snapping from behind the caravan. Gwen paused and they all listened, but it didn't come back.

"As a girl," Mum began, "Gwen wore two braids. When she declared her Trace, she joined them together one, as according to tradition. Now, in keeping with that same tradition, I will shear off the braid that Gwenli has worn since her Trace. Now, as the braid falls, she shows the world the commitment she is making to my son, Ellison Blackworth. "

A cheer went up, and Ell saw his mother murmur something in Gwen's ear. The girl smiled and nodded.

His mother lowered the scissors to Gwenli's braid, and a hush went over the caravan. Ell could've sworn he heard whispers from somewhere behind the circle but dismissed it as the wind. With one motion, Mum cut the braid.

Ellison heard a *snip*, and then it was done.

His mother held up the blonde braid, free from Gwenli's head. As she raised it, the crowd cheered thunderously.

Gwen was beaming from ear to ear. As Ell looked at her for the first time, her hair hung around her neck and fell right above her shoulders. She was beautiful. More beautiful than she'd been on the night they declared their Traces and more beautiful than on the night they'd first kissed.

As he stared, Gwen opened her lips and mouthed something to him. He didn't catch it the first time—one of the children ran between them, obscuring her face. She repeated it, and this time he understood. *I want to stay here,* she said.

The caravan? he mouthed back.

She smiled from across the fire and nodded, her short blonde hair swaying about her chin. "Forever," she called.

He stared at her, and she stared right back, and at that moment, while everyone around them got up to dance, while someone started to play a tune on a lute or fiddle, it was like everything else stopped. All that mattered was the two of them together.

A cold voice rent the air in two.

"Oh, isn't that just wonderful!"

It came from outside the firelight. It was high, almost…amused. Something about it sent Ellison into a sweat.

"Such a romantic couple," it drawled. Half of the caravan froze, looking for the source—the other half continued dancing and joking.

Ell locked eyes with his father, who stepped forward. "Who's there?" Papa called into the night.

"Oh, just me."

A man stepped into the light. He wearing black robes stepped into the light.

Ellison's breath caught in his throat. By now, the entire caravan was frozen still.

"Who…who are you?" Papa asked, placing himself between the man and the children.

"Gentlemen, let's introduce ourselves," he smiled.

From out of the shadows, two dozen rough-looking men stepped forward, brandishing blades and spears.

Ellison heard his mother gasp and put a hand to her mouth. His own heart was pounding in his chest, but not because of the gang.

He knew why the man's voice had scared him so. He'd heard it once before—so had Gwen. Across the fire, her eyes were locked with Ellison's.

It's him. It's the man who didn't burn.

The man from Aelos.

Chapter 17
Darkness, pt. II

Ellison's breath caught in his throat, and his stomach dropped.

"Don't worry, everyone," the man said. "I don't want to *kill* you—though I'm not opposed to it, so don't try anything dangerous."

"What do you want with us?" Grandpa Emory called out.

The man smiled. "You all are merchants, right?"

They gave no response.

" Are you going to rob us?" asked Gwenli's mother, her voice breaking.

"No, no," he smiled. "No. Well, sort of."

"What—what do you mean?"

"You sell odds and ends. Trinkets," the man said. "I sell...well...it's complicated."

People, Ellison realized distantly. *He sells people into slavery, like he almost did to Gwen that night.* Looking around, he watched the truth dawn one by one on the rest of the caravanners.

"Now you get it," the man cackled, clapping his hands together. "There's no use being dramatic, I suppose. I sell people. I will sell you all, too."

"You'll do no such thing!" Grandpa Em shouted, his face red.

The slavers moved between the dark man and him, but the man waved them back. "Let me," he murmured.

"Leave now," Grandpa Emory growled. "You will *not* break our family."

The man waited for a moment before smiling. "Step back, old man."

Grandpa Em didn't move.

The slaver burst forward. Grandpa Em tried to leap away, but his knee gave out and he collapsed to the ground. In a blur, the man was atop him. With a flick of his wrist, he drew a knife and slit Grandpa Emory's throat.

"No!" Ellison roared, starting forward. There was a hand on his wrist—Gwen's, jerking him backwards.

"Not yet," she whispered, her eyes wide. "Please."

He was dead. His grandfather, a man who'd held him as a child, who'd helped him pick his Trace, suffocating to death in the grass. Ellison's mother started to cry, as did a few of the younger girls nearby. Papa was frozen, barely breathing.

"Oh, well," the man shrugged. "He wasn't worth much anyways." He turned to address the caravanners, all looking on in terror. "Now, as I said, you all are going to help me turn a nice profit. If you decide not to cooperate," he gestured to Grandpa Em, now still and dead, "well, I don't advise it. All of you, put your hands in the air."

Slowly, Ellison's father raised his hands. The rest of the caravan followed suit.

"Good," the man said. "Now, just stay where you are, and we'll make sure nobody is hurt."

The slavers procured manacles from pouches at their side. One by one, they began fastening cuffs on the wrists of Ellison's friends and family.

I refuse to let them take this away from us.

The chains clicked shut around little Lief's tiny wrists, and he whimpered in pain.

I refuse to let our lives end in one night.

They pinned his mother and father, too. Nobody put up a fight.

Ell tensed up, adrenaline rushing in preparation for what he was about to do.

Gwen already knew. She grabbed his wrist. "Don't. Please."

"I have to," he whispered.

"Please," she begged, tears coming to her eyes. "Don't do it."

He lowered his hands to his sides and kissed her.

"Hey!" one of the slavers cried. "Hands over your head!"

"I have to," he repeated, turning to face the slaver. Slowly, he raised his hands above his head.

When one of the men came around reached up to grab his wrists, Ellison exploded. He brought his knee up into the man's stomach, sending him backwards into the blazing fire.

The adrenaline gave him purpose. Ell threw himself into another nearby slaver, who fell and lost his sword. Ellison darted down, grabbing the blade into his own hands.

Oh!" the leader cackled. "We've got a fighter!"

As a few of the slavers turned towards him, growling, Ellison hefted the sword in his grip. It felt different than he'd imagined as a boy—heavier.

Three slavers came after him slowly, spears out in a semi-circle. Ell tensed, rocking on his heels, then exploded again.

He thrust the blade to the left. The target evaded easily. Using the momentum of his attack, he swept his sword at the slaver in the center. It connected with his thigh and the man hit the ground, clutching at his leg.

Ellison stepped towards the bonfire, barely ducking an attack. With as much speed as he could bear, he swung his boot into the flames, flinging embers and coals towards his attackers.

They screamed out in pain, dropping their weapons to pat out the flames. Out of the corner of his eye, Ellison saw a few of the other caravanners use his distraction to shove their captors into the bonfire. He swung his blade and severed a slaver's head.

Before he could turn, a thunderous force hit him in the small of his back, knocking the wind from his lungs. Ell collapsed to his stomach, sword flying from his grasp.

Persevere. He gasped and scrambled to his feet before the man could kick him again.

The slaver came at him with a sword. Ellison's first instinct was to turn tail and run, but he steeled himself, letting the mantra repeat in his head. *Persevere.*

The swordsman swung his blade to sever Ellison's neck. He ducked and sprung off his heels, grabbing the man by his waist and tearing him to the ground. Like days before in Enthcas, Ell pinned him with his knees and punched until the attacker had stopped struggling. *Persevere.*

He'd lost his sword. By now, the entire caravan was fighting back. Ellison searched for his parents and Gwenli but couldn't spot them amidst the chaos. *We can win. We outnumber them, we—*

Across the fire, he saw the leader, the man from Aelos, holding a knife to a struggling girl.

Gwen.

The man locked eyes with Ellison. "Stop the fighting," he called. "Or she dies!"

There was no hesitation in his mind. "Stop!" Ellison shouted over the chaos, waving his arms. "Surrender!" He pulled a caravanner free of a slaver's grip. "All of you, stop fighting back!"

They couldn't hear him. He ran at Gwenli's father, struggling on the ground with a dark-haired attacker, and flung him backwards off the man. "Don't fight! Stop! He's got Gwen! You have to stop now!"

Ell and Gwen's father took up the cry together. "Stop! Surrender! Put your weapons down!"

Now it took hold. Finally, the caravan glanced over, saw Gwenli, and froze. Weapons were dropped, and, a thin quiet laid over the night once again. Ellison exhaled.

"Very good!" the man cackled, still holding Gwenli by the throat. "Very good, boy! A warrior boy, it seems. Very good…you'll make a fine soldier, I think. Though I can't say the same for the rest of you," he laughed.

"Let her go," Ellison called, pointing to Gwenli. "Please. What do you want us to do?"

The man thought for a moment, his grip tight around Gwen's throat. "Hmm…about two minutes ago, I just wanted a nice, peaceful transaction, but now I feel a little differently. I think now I want to play a game."

"What?" Ellison panted. "Please, don't hurt anyone else. Just kill me. Nobody else needs to be involved in this."

"Oh, but that's what makes it so fun," the man pouted.

"Why—why are you here?" Gwen grunted, jerking against his grip.

The man cackled. "Ah, there it is. I knew you'd ask."

"Ask? Ask what?" Papa asked, looking from Ellison to Gwenli to the man.

"We've met him before, Papa," Ell explained, his eyes locked on the man who had Gwen at knifepoint. "He tried to capture us four years ago, in Aelos."

"No, no," the assailant gasped. "Not capture you, never *capture* you! That was never my intention…"

"Then what did you want?"

The man smiled slyly. "Well, I'm afraid I can't say that…at least not tonight."

Ellison fought back a shiver. "Then take us," he called. "Please, you can let everyone else go."

The man clicked his tongue. "Things have gotten a little more…complicated…since that night. I'm afraid that would make things too easy."

"Let me go, you monster," Gwen spat, still in his grip.

The man looked down at her in surprise. "Oh, she's fiery. I can see why you like this one, warrior boy. Oh, this will make things *much* more interesting."

"What are you talking about?" Ellison shouted in frustration.

"You'll see," he murmured. "In time."

"What do you want?"

"You know, I'm used to folks fighting back," he went on. "But I'll admit, I was surprised when you lashed out. After that night in Aelos…you practically gave this one to me, didn't you?"

Ellison flashed back to that night. The high, maniacal laughter. Gwen's cries for help and his terror—*'I'm just a boy. I can't stop a grown man.'* He'd failed her that night.

He would not fail her again.

The man paused, then smiled again. "Come, warrior boy. I want to play a game." He tightened his grip on Gwen, whose eyes were locked on Ell.

"It's going to be okay, love," Ellison called. "Just hold on."

The man chuckled. "Oh, that's sweet. Warrior boy, tonight, you hurt a lot of my own friends. So I think it's only fair that I hurt some of yours." He twisted Gwenli around so she was face to face with him. "Hello, dear," he muttered, looking her all over. "Sorry about this." He placed his dagger, still red with Grandpa Em's blood, at her jaw.

Chapter 18
Persevere

"NO!" Ellison roared, running towards him.

"Ah!" the slaver shouted, shifting the knife towards Gwen's throat. "I could just kill her if you'd like…"

He froze.

"There we are," the man smiled. "That's what I thought."

Ellison watched as he took the knife and brought it back to Gwenli's cheek.

"You have such beautiful skin, my love," the man crooned. "It almost makes me jealous…"

Gwen whimpered, biting her lip. She locked eyes with Ellison, who stood frozen in place.

The knife broke flesh. Her scream tore the night and made Ellison flinch. His hands shook, but he stood still. *Persevere.*

The man dug the knife deeper into the soft, supple flesh of her cheek, then began to cut upward. Gwen screamed aloud. Ell could swear that he heard his own name among her shrieks. He opened his mouth to shout, but he didn't know what to say. His heart burned with cold fury.

The man jerked his wrist upwards and the knife travelled the length of Gwen's face, ending at her forehead. She finally broke, bringing both hands up to clutch her bloody face. The man giggled and kicked her to the grass, where she collapsed.

Ellison stepped towards her, but the man shouted a warning, and he stepped back again. "You've played your game. Please, just chain us up and let it be over!"

"Bring me his parents!" the slaver shouted.

No. Firion, no.

The other men glanced over the caravanners, but didn't move. "Which ones are those?"

Please, no. Don't.

"Idiots," the leader grumbled. He pointed directly at Mum and Papa. "Those two. See? No, not them—them. Yes, bring them to me."

Two slavers dragged Hanik and Issela Blackworth forward to the robed man, who grabbed them both by the collar.

"Please," Ellison begged. "Anything—I will do anything for you. Just don't hurt them."

"Oh, he's so *desperate*," the man cackled. "Alright, I'll only kill one. Oh, but how to decide?" He put a finger to his lips. "Oh, I know! You'll have to tell me which one."

No. No, no.

"If you don't choose, I'll slaughter them both. But if you play the game, if you make a choice, the bloodshed can end there."

"Please, don't—"

"Ah!" the slaver cut him off. "Do you have a decision?"

There's nothing you can do.

An old fear settled over Ellison. He was unable to speak.

"Come on, warrior boy!"

You are trapped. Every option you have will end in bloodshed. You have failed them.

109

You swore you would never fail them again, after that night in Aelos.

Tears began to roll down Ellison's cheeks.

"Oh, is he *crying*?" the man cried.

You can do nothing.

Of course I can—

He will kill them both. You have failed the caravan and your parents.

"Fine, then," the man shrugged. "I suppose I can help force a decision. Someone give me a hammer."

One of the slavers drew a war hammer from his belt and tossed it to the man. He flung Ellison's mother into the grass and pinned her with his knee, pushing Papa down next to her. "One last chance, boy!"

Ellison knew he needed to speak, but he couldn't. He didn't know how to say, what to say...

"Alright, then." The man raised his hammer over his head.

And then, with lightning speed, he brought it down on Papa's kneecap.

Deep, frantic screams rent the air. "Ellison!" Papa screamed. "Please, son!"

"Ready to make a choice, warrior boy?"

He was frozen silent.

This is your fault. How will you live with yourself in the future?

I have to—

There is nothing you can do.

"Fine!" The man sighed. "Round two, old man!"

"Don't listen to the voice, Ellison!" Papa screamed.

The black-robed man drove the hammer down on his father's other knee. Ell heard a crunching sound. *You don't understand, Papa. I'm so sorry.*

"Please, son! Do it." The voice belonged to his father. "Pick me! I know you're afraid, but remember," he choked on a breath and coughed blood on the grass.

The monstrous man in black stood now, tossed the hammer aside, and placed his heel over Papa's knee. "Next chance. This one'll hurt!"

You have killed them both.

I have killed them both. I have failed Gwenli and now my parents.

Persevere.

The man placed his boot on Papa's shattered knee and twisted his heel, grinding the splintered bone against itself. Papa screamed and vomited in the grass, his hands clawing at the dirt. "Please, Ellison! The loudest voice—the loudest voice is the one in your head! Remember! Please—"

The voice in my head.

You are not in control of me. I refuse to be paralyzed by fear. "STOP!"

The robed man paused and looked up at Ellison. "Oh?"

"Stop," Ell repeated. "Stop hurting them. I'll choose."

The man laughed. "Go ahead."

"Take my—take my father. Please."

The slaver drew his knife again. "That's what I thought you'd say." He stepped closer to Papa, then…around him. Towards Ellison's mother, laying frozen in fear a few paces away.

"No!" Ell shouted. "I chose! I played your game! I made a choice, didn't I?"

The man giggled. "Yes, I suppose you did. But here's the thing, boy." He knelt right by Issela and held the knife high. "I don't care." Without another breath, he rammed the blade straight into Mum's throat and twisted it there.

His mother screamed, a wet, terrified shriek.

"NO!" Ellison roared. She jerked and spasmed, trying to force air into her lungs.

Look what you—

111

Ellison snapped. He ran at the man.

Laughing, the monster spun out of the way and Ellison dove into empty space, collapsing onto the ground.

"Put them in the wagons!" the leader called. "I'll handle this one...."

The slavers grabbed up the women, men, and children and started dragging them away to the wagons. As Ell pushed himself up to his knees, he heard Gwenli screaming above the clamor.

"Ellison!" she cried. "Ellison! Help me! Please, help me!" She was struggling against her captors, but they overpowered her. In the dim light, he could see that the right side of her face and neck was covered in blood, her newly cut hair soaked red. "Save me, Ell! You promised!"

He was helpless. For the second time in his life, he was watching Gwenli pulled away from him, kicking frantically and screaming for his help. Ell tried to stand, but the man kicked him to the ground again.

"Stay alive, Gwen!" he shouted to the darkness. "I'll find you! Keep my father sa—"

There was a blunt pain to the back of his head and everything went black.

Chapter 19
Lord Blackworth, pt. III

When he'd awoken, the rest of the caravanners were gone. The slavers had led him, bound and gagged, across the countryside for what was probably a full prayer. He'd spent it starved and dehydrated and alone.

The man hadn't reappeared except for once. They'd stopped on the shore somewhere, Ellison blindfolded. He'd heard the man's slimy, silky voice speaking to someone else. The next thing he'd known, the slavers were gone, and Ellison was on a boat. He'd been sold into service of the Vahzese Military.

He had been supposed to marry Gwenli.

He had been supposed to lead the caravan in his father's place.

He had been supposed to have children and watch them grow.

Instead, Ellison was sold into military service in a small, bloodthirsty nation called Vahzal, far away from Caraspen. Far away from everything he'd ever known.

It was not the heroic life of he'd dreamt of. He was not Lord Blackworth, he had no shining ranks of soldiers to lead. His entire battalion was made of criminals, outlaws, and slaves—they were used as shields on the front lines for the other soldiers.

Ellison, however, was not so easily disposed of.

He became the best soldier in the battalion. He trained with the sword and shield, with the bow and arrow, with the spear. After a year, he was the most experienced soldier in the battalion, and they hated him for it. He wanted to die, probably more so than any of the other men who were sold into service of Battalion Eighteen, but he never let himself. Perhaps he was too good of a soldier. Perhaps he was still holding onto the hope that he'd get free and find Gwen one day. And perhaps he had been scared off of giving up by a cautionary tale he'd once told a young boy.

But through the pain, one word kept him alive. Whether he wanted to or not, it pushed him through the suffering he endured daily, both emotional and physical.

Persevere.

APPENDIX: LIST OF CELESTIM

Cynicism
Envy
Curiosity
Infatuation
Vigilance
Love
Joy
Altruism
Passion
Peace
Patience
Dedication
Perseverance
Bravery
Temerity
Ambition
Loyalty
Awe
Humility
Justice
Honesty
Chivalry
Rationality